First published 2015 by
Mabecron Books
42 Drake Circus
Plymouth
PL4 8AB

Printed in Italy
ISBN 9780957256064

www.mabecronbooks.co.uk

CAPTURED!

The
INCREDIBLE TRUE STORY OF
THOMAS PELLOW

Published by

MABECRON BOOKS

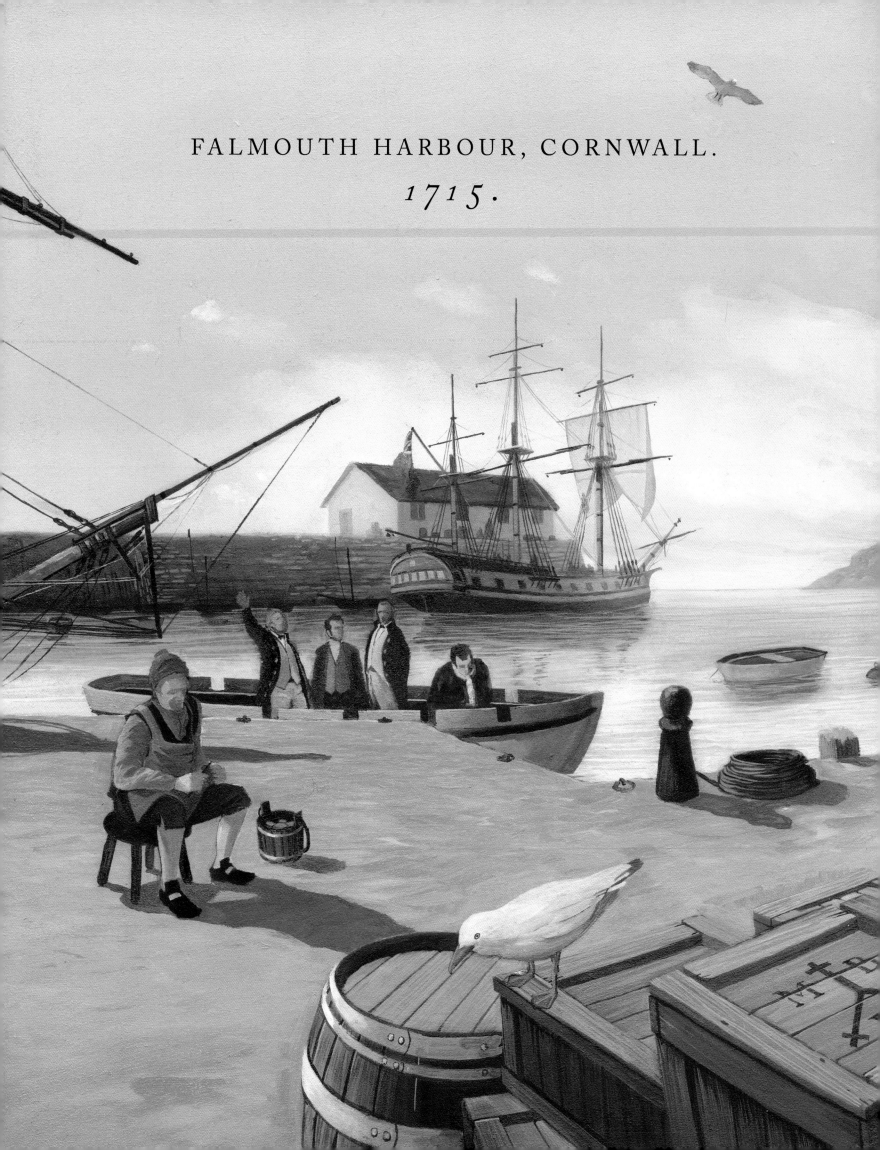

FALMOUTH HARBOUR, CORNWALL.
1715.

'Hoist that there sail, Tommy lad!' shouted Captain John Pellow.
'Yes sir!' shouted young Thomas Pellow.

Thomas pulled hard on one of the ropes that hung from the rigging, and watched as the sail was raised high into the Cornish sky. The ship was a hive of activity. The members of the crew were dashing around the deck, making their final preparations to leave. Thomas felt a bit silly in his sailor's uniform, but rules were rules. Slowly but surely the ship started to move. Its journey had begun.

'This is your last chance to get off boy,' said the Captain, who also happened to be Thomas's uncle.
'Not a chance Uncle … I mean … Captain.'
'Good. Now get up that mast then lad. We have work to do.'

Everyone he knew would be warmly tucked up in bed. Thomas wished his mother and father and sisters were there to wave him off. They had given him a party the night before, for his trip at sea would last many weeks. He had to beg them to let him go. They said it was too dangerous for an eleven-year-old boy to be so long at sea, especially with all the things that might go wrong. But they knew Thomas was a boy ready for adventure so eventually they had agreed, making him promise to be extra, *extra* careful. That morning Thomas had been almost sick with excitement. He desperately wanted to see the world outside of Cornwall and now it was finally going to happen. He had run the two mile journey to the harbour without looking back once. And now he was here, on a ship, bound for his first adventure. It was a dream come true.

The boat picked up a little speed. Thomas looked back at the higgledy-piggledy houses which appeared beautiful in the misty light of the early morning. He waved in the direction of his family home. Thomas wasn't to know he wouldn't see it again for a very long time.

THE year was 1715 and the good ship *Francis* had been at sea for several weeks. The ship was full of pilchards to deliver to the Italian port of Genoa. As well as eleven-year-old Thomas Pellow and his Uncle, Captain John Pellow, six other men made up the crew: George Barnicoat, Thomas Goodman, Lewis Davis, Briant Clarke, John Dunnal and John Crimes. Thomas found the work onboard very hard, but he was having the time of his life. He was particularly fond of the sea-salty smell of his cabin at night time. He adored curling up in the rough canvas hammock while the waves rocked him to sleep. The whispering wind and the caws of the gulls that accompanied the groan of the creaking ship filled his dreams.

The crew had successfully delivered their pilchards to Genoa and replaced the incoming cargo with all kinds of goods which would be sold back in England. On the return journey they soon reached the Bay of Biscay - the roughest and most dangerous part of the Atlantic Ocean – sitting just between France and Spain. The day was warm and hazy. The ship was cutting through the water like sharp scissors through blue paper. Thomas was at the top of the mast. He felt a bit wobbly, but the view was incredible and he loved to feel the wind blowing his hair.

Thomas turned his head and looked out to the horizon. It was quite empty. And then, suddenly, it was not. A boat appeared, and then another. They were getting bigger by the moment. Thomas instinctively knew something wasn't right. He wriggled down the mast to find his uncle who was below decks talking to John Crimes.

'What is it Tommy?' said the Captain.
'Ships ahead. Two of them, coming this way!' panted Thomas.

THEY ran up the ladder to the side of the ship and looked out to sea. The rest of the crew could sense the danger brewing. Uncle John pulled out his telescope, his hands trembling. A ship filled the lens. He moved the instrument to the left and spotted the other one. Both ships had plain flags, but in that moment they were brought down. Captain Pellow watched as they were replaced with ragged black ones filled with pictures of big curved swords.

'Oh no,' exclaimed his Uncle.

'What is it?' said Thomas.

'Pirates Tommy, pirates!'

Thomas felt his knees turn to jelly.

'Pirates!' roared Captain John Pellow to the crew around him. He knew they hadn't packed any weapons to defend themselves. Thomas felt his uncle's hands on his shoulders, gripping him tightly.

'This will not end well Tommy. Do whatever it takes to stay alive. These pirates are bad men. They aren't here to steal our boat or our monies, these pirates steal *people*.'

'Hide Tommy lad. Now! Hide!'

THOMAS was frozen to the spot with fear. The pirates were approaching fast. Whichever way he looked he could see danger. The pirates were leaning over the sides of their boats. They had shaved heads and bare arms that were smeared with blood. They waved pistols and long curved swords. They were shrieking and screaming; their blood-curdling cries caught on the wind and swirled around Thomas's ears. He started to cry. He had heard stories about these pirates; awful, horrible stories.

'Tommy! Run!' shouted John Crimes.

Thomas Pellow came alive and ran below deck as fast as he could. He hid in the pantry among the barrels of food supplies. He closed his eyes and held his breath.

He waited.

And waited.

And waited.

He shook with fear.

It wasn't long before the pirates found him.

THEY dragged him by the hair and threw him on board a rowing boat. Thomas Pellow had been captured. He had been stolen. He was pushed onto the deck of the second ship and joined the many other captives who all looked sick and miserable. For days Thomas lived amongst them, below decks with the rats. The pirates hit and whipped him. They pointed their swords towards him and shouted strange words into his face.

Once the pirates had plundered enough boats, they began the return journey to Morocco. There they would sell the slaves and collect their money. It was a long journey in foul weather. As they approached the port of Salé the pirates were surprised to see a ship, not far away from them, on their starboard side. It was a huge English vessel with lots of cannon. The pirates panicked, thinking they might lose their valuable cargo. All they could do was try to reach port as quickly as possible. The weather grew steadily worse. Thomas could feel the angry waves shaking the boat. He sat shivering in his dark, filthy prison. The sound of the pirates bellowing instructions to each other turned his blood to ice but he could not understand a word.

THEN there came an almighty crash and bang ... an explosion of splinters ... an earthquake of ripping timber. The boat moaned and groaned as it started to fall apart. The pirates had misread the tides. The water was too shallow for their vessel and it had run aground. They tried desperately to rescue the situation, but the waves and the weather were fast reducing the stranded boat to matchsticks. Both slaves and pirates had no choice but to dive into the sea and swim for shore.

THOMAS expected to drown. He was a terrible swimmer and was gulping mouthfuls of sea water. 'Please help me!' shouted Thomas to Lewis Davis, the closest shipmate to him. Lewis shook his head sadly and swam away from the terrified boy. A broken mast from the pirate ship floated near to Thomas and by some miracle he was able to reach it. He clung on tightly while the waves carried him to shore.

The slaves who had not drowned were easily rounded up and put in chains. They were sent to a deep, foul smelling pit with a barred metal roof. They were exhausted, terrified and starving.

Some days later they were dragged from their prison and lined up by their captors. One of the men spoke English and told them that they were going on a long journey which would take them to the pirates' leader, the Sultan Ismail. Once there he would decide whether to buy them, or have them killed.

THEIR journey took them through the Salé woodlands. It lasted four long days and a great many miles were covered. To Thomas's astonishment the woods were full of animals, the likes of which he could scarcely have imagined. There were leopards and huge wild hogs, lions, tigers, and spectacular birds. Thomas thought he would be eaten alive at any moment.

THE marketplace bordered a great palace. It was even more frightening than the forest. The crowds swarmed around the slaves like vultures. Thomas felt like a strange creature in a strange land. As the Sultan approached, the atmosphere changed. Everyone feared him. He had complete control of all his land and the seas around it, and was known for being very cruel. He was a powerful man, cunning and clever and he led a ferocious army which was devoted to him.

The Sultan made his grand entrance and took his seat high above the courtyard. Slowly and carefully he examined the slaves. He looked Thomas up and down. Thomas held his breath and trembled but he looked straight into the Sultan's dark eyes. It was decided that all of the slaves would be bought. Thomas was handed over to the Sultan's favourite son while the rest were sent to the dungeons. Thomas watched in despair as his uncle disappeared from sight.

THOMAS was treated very badly by his new master. He was held in chains, given hardly any food or water, and grew very weak. It was the worst time of his life. Only the dream of one day seeing his family again kept his spirits alive.

After several weeks he was released from his chains and put to task. He worked in the beautiful gardens of the Sultan's wife. She liked to take a walk among the flowers, so the slaves made sure that everything was perfect for her. If she ever arrived unannounced and surprised them, the slaves had to hide or lie on the ground with their eyes closed.

One day she did arrive without notice and she spotted Thomas before he was able to hide. She was very taken by the handsome young boy who stood in front of her and demanded that he be sent to work in her private palace.

THE Sultan agreed to his wife's demand and Thomas's life began to improve a little. He was given more food and water and a comfortable room to sleep in. He shared his sleeping quarters with six other slave boys and two young lions, which Thomas found *very* odd indeed.

DESPITE life becoming easier, Thomas was still very frightened. He saw the Sultan be unspeakably cruel, sometimes slicing off the heads of slaves who angered him. He expected something dreadful to happen at any moment.

He was a clever boy and quickly learned the Moroccan language, and over the years developed an ability to speak many of the different languages he encountered.

As the years passed, Thomas grew from a frightened eleven-year-old boy into an accomplished and respected young adult. Thomas gained the Sultan's trust over time, though one particular evening had been a turning point …

THE Sultan had given Thomas a gun and told him he must stand guard at a secret doorway into the palace. He was to shoot anybody who tried to enter.

That evening Thomas was guarding the door as instructed when he heard a loud bang.

'Let me in!' boomed a voice from the other side of the door.

'No,' said Thomas, 'I cannot let you pass. If you try to enter I will shoot you.'

'You will let me enter!' demanded the voice again.

'No, the Sultan himself has given orders. I must shoot anybody who tries to enter.'

'But I am the Sultan! Now let me in you wretched slave.'

Thomas was distraught. What if this was an imposter pretending to be the Sultan? But if it was the Sultan and he didn't let him pass then he would surely be punished. He didn't know what to do, but finally made up his mind.

'I serve the Sultan and follow his orders to the letter. If you refuse to leave, I will fire this gun through the door.'

'How dare you. I am the Sultan and I order you to open this door!'

Hands shaking, Thomas pointed the gun at the middle of the large door in front of him.

BANG!

He fired the gun towards the door as ordered by his ruler. He heard only silence as he stood with eyes wide, awaiting his fate. After a while, he was seized by the Sultan's guards, their fierce expressions giving nothing away. This had to be the end for Thomas.

But to his surprise the Sultan was sitting in his chair, waiting for him. He glared menacingly at Thomas and again Thomas returned his gaze. Loudly and with great exaggeration the Sultan began to laugh, and then to applaud Thomas for his outstanding service and loyal stubbornness. It was indeed the Sultan who had stood at the doorway testing his young protégé. He was very impressed at the bravery shown by the young Thomas and gave him a gift of a fine white horse. From that moment on he entrusted him with many more tasks.

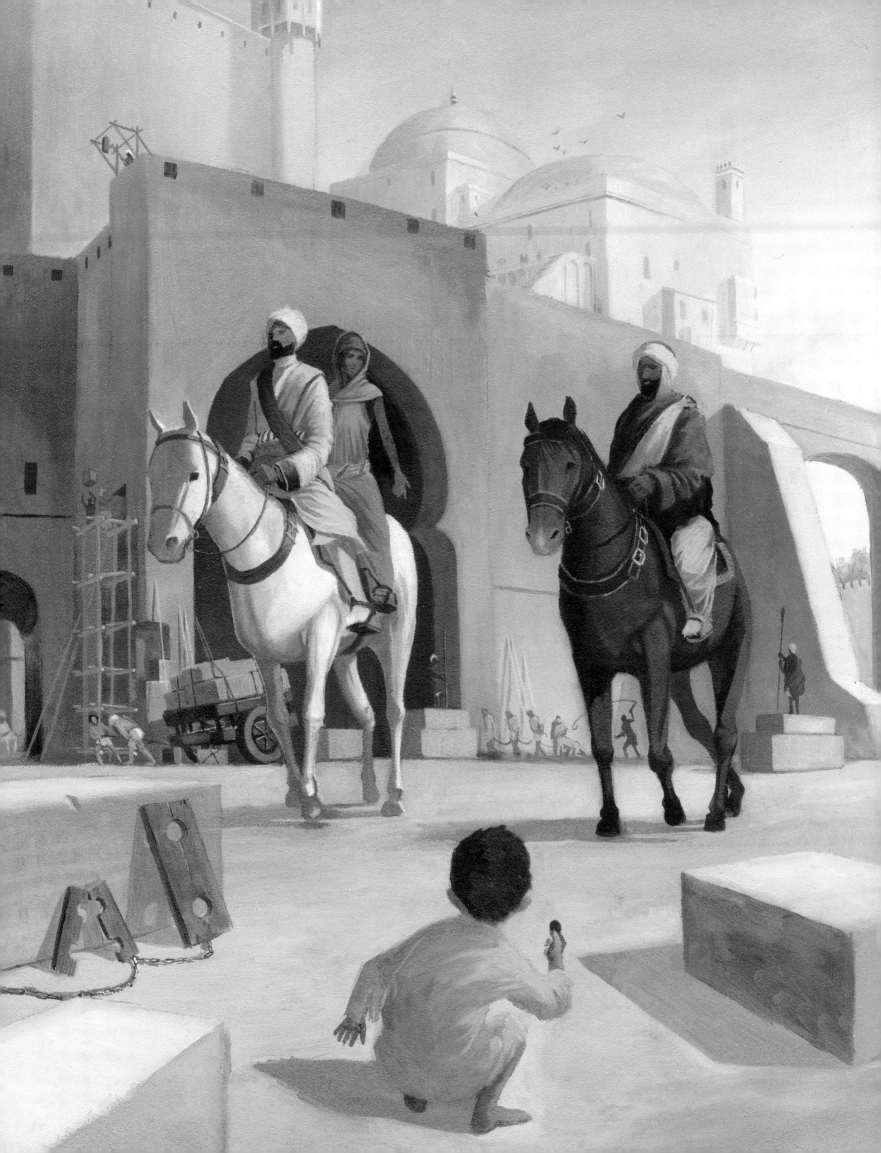

Thomas had grown tall and strong, and was given fine robes which he wore with great ease. Around his twentieth birthday he began to act as a translator to the Sultan. He attended many great feasts and saw riches that dazzled his eyes. He was given a house and land, and even money of his own. Thomas married, and his wife gave birth to a beautiful baby girl.

He was still a slave however, and was unable to help his old shipmates or his Uncle John. They remained in dungeons by night and were forced to break their backs in hard labour by day – gruelling long hours in the blistering heat, without enough food or water. Eventually his uncle, like many of the others, succumbed to a foreign fever and died in captivity. Thomas was filled with anguish and helplessness.

At the age of twenty-eight, Thomas was given the honour of leading the Sultan's fighting missions abroad. He was initially alarmed because it would mean great danger and he was far from confident about his own fighting abilities. He was ordered to take the Sultan's army high into the Atlas Mountains where, in the snow and freezing fog, they fought the enemies of the Sultan.

On his second mission he marched with thirty thousand men and twelve thousand camels across the Sahara desert, passing the bones of long dead travellers along the way. He was often shot or stabbed in the many battles, but somehow he always survived. However, he knew that one day his luck would run out.

When Thomas was thirty-four years old, and while away on yet another dangerous expedition, he was sent news that his wife and child had died. Thomas was devastated. In all the time he had been captured, he had heard no word of his family back home in Cornwall. He now felt desperately sad and alone. Escaping the clutches of the Sultan had always felt like an impossible dream as there were spies and informers everywhere. But Thomas had had enough. He needed to take action or he would be trapped in Morocco for the rest of his life.

As fate would have it, a chance meeting was to give Thomas the courage he needed. While he was returning with his men after a particularly exhausting mission, a woman caught his eye. She was dressed curiously and carried a green cane. She stared at him hard, refusing to look away.

'Go away please,' said the weary Thomas but she continued her intense gaze, making him feel very uncomfortable.

'I can tell the secrets of your heart.'

'Are you a fortune teller?' asked Thomas, letting his curiosity get the better of him.

'Let me read for you. I will tell you things that will help you.'

Thomas gave her some money and she drew the tip of her cane upwards in an arc before pulling it across her left palm.

'You are a stranger here … You want to leave … You want to go somewhere you can feel at peace …'

Thomas was stunned. He could only stare into her eyes, wondering what else she could see.

'If you make your escape, you will succeed.' said this strange woman.

'But how can I? It is too dangerous, and what have I to return to? My parents will likely be dead and I will be alone again.'

'You will survive,' she insisted, 'your mother is alive and well, and she is waiting for you.'

'Impossible! That is impossible, I can't believe you.'

'Escape and you will see your family again. Be brave.'

Thomas was taken aback. His tears flowed at the thought of returning home. The fortune-teller tapped her cane on the ground and moved away, leaving Thomas to his thoughts and emotions.

Within hours he began to plan his escape.

OVER the years Thomas Pellow's skin had turned dark and he spoke the Arabic languages as well as he spoke English. He knew he would not draw suspicion if he were to travel alone through the countryside. He was stationed at the Kasbah on the night he plucked up his courage. The moon shone brightly to guide his escape and without alerting anyone he stealthily exited the heavily guarded fortification.

He walked without stopping for several days. The road was dangerous and he was in constant fear of spies. The journey to the sea was hard. He was attacked by the vicious gangs that roamed the wilderness and was robbed of many of his possessions. But as long as he had his sword and his wits he was able to continue. The nights were bitterly cold and his clothing did little to protect him. He had hardly any food to eat so often he would ask for help from the houses he passed. In one simple home a kind person offered him salted locusts; huge fat insects as big as his thumb. He was so hungry he closed his eyes and took a bite. It was crunchy and surprisingly delicious!

AFTER countless days of walking he finally arrived at the port of Willadia. His journey had been long and bruising. His body was aching and broken. But he never once gave up hope. He sensed the nearness of his freedom and this gave him the courage to continue.

At Willadia he met an Irishman called Captain Toobin who listened as Thomas told his incredible story. The Sultan's spies and informers could be anywhere so the Captain decided that he would hide Thomas below decks for the duration of the journey. Eleven long days later they weighed anchor in Gibraltar. Once there Thomas was able to contact another man whose ship was bound for London. Captain John Peacock offered to help Thomas on the next stage of his long voyage. He hid him, amongst the barrels, on board his ship the *Euphrates*.

Hidden away below the decks of the *Euphrates*, Thomas found it cramped and hard to breathe. It was much like his experience of twenty-three years earlier when he was packed in like a pilchard with all of the other slaves. Again, a mighty storm raged and Thomas was terrified that the boat would fall apart. But this time the boat stayed in one piece, continuing onwards to his homeland. The journey had lasted a total of thirty-one agonising days.

IRELAND

GREAT BRITAIN

PRUSSIA

POLAND-LITHUANIA

○ LONDON

PENRYN ○

BAY OF BISCAY

FRANCE

HUNGARY

PORTUGAL

SPAIN

ITALY

GENOA ○

GIBRALTAR ○

SALÉ ○

WILLADIA ○

MOROCCO

LONDON was impossibly busy and he wandered the unfamiliar streets feeling very out of place. He found himself at the office of the Moroccan Ambassador, where he was warmly welcomed. The Ambassador listened to his astonishing story while Thomas gratefully enjoyed a meal, which consisted of the food he had grown so used to in the Sultan's palace. The Ambassador helped Thomas to locate a ship which would take him home to Cornwall; the good ship *Truro*, sailed by a kindly man called Captain Francis. Thomas found it comforting that this Captain shared the same name as the ship he had set sail on as a young boy. Life was strange!

THE journey was quick as the wind blew in the direction of home. Thomas again climbed the mast to feel the wind on his face. Eventually his beloved Cornwall appeared on the horizon and he could visualise the fleets of boats in the harbour. He could almost feel the street cobbles under his feet and best of all, he imagined sitting at the table with his family eating his mother's homemade bread.

As the *Truro* sailed into Falmouth, his heart thumped with excitement. Everything looked the same, but somehow it all seemed smaller. Thomas took his leave of the Captain and jumped down from the boat. Again he ran the two mile journey, retracing the steps of his younger self; the boy who had been so eager to embark on a great adventure.

THOMAS drew closer to home and a crowd began to gather around him. He stopped a woman in the street.

'Madam, does the Pellow family still live here?'

The woman shrieked. She had never seen a man like Thomas before. She ran from him, clutching her hat to her head. The crowd was amazed by his fine robes, his jewellery, his exotic headscarf, his curved Moroccan sword; he had kept it by him for so many years, he had quite forgotten about it.

'Where are you from?'

'What do you want from us?'

'Are you a prince from the East?'

Thomas turned around and around and saw only wide eyes, some scared, some wondrous. For a moment he wished that he was back in Morocco.

He felt again like a strange foreign slave in the marketplace, with everyone shouting at him in excitement. But Thomas was a free man, headed for home. He thought of his family and pushed on towards the people.

'Silence!' he commanded. The crowd stopped talking immediately.

'My name is Thomas Pellow. I was born here, thirty-four years ago.
When I was a boy of eleven our Cornish vessel, the *Francis*, was
captured by pirates near Spain. I was kept as a slave in Morocco,
but I escaped and now I have returned home. If it is still my home?'

The crowd gasped …

'Tommy Pellow! Lord preserve me!' shouted an elderly woman.
'Your mother is still here Sir, my flower, still in the very same house.
We all thought you had died long ago. Come with me my handsome prince!'

Thomas followed the woman as they walked to his childhood home. Before he even got there, the woman shouted,

'There! There she is my Prince, Mr Pellow.'

Mrs Pellow could not believe the scene she was witnessing; a huge man with a thick beard and colourful robes, and behind him a sea of people bobbing with excitement. Thomas was shocked to see his elderly mother, grown haggard with age and worry. She could hardly recognise her own boy, grown so different under a foreign sun.

'I've come home Mother,' said Thomas.

'But ... you ... but ... how ...' stuttered Mrs Pellow in disbelief.

Before she could fully understand what was happening Thomas picked her up, hugging her tightly just as she had hugged him twenty-three years earlier.

THAT night the people of the town welcomed Thomas back among them. He told them stories of pirates and sultans and adventures on the high seas. He told them of shootings and stabbings and beheadings, of being held in dungeons and starved to near death. He described the wild animals and huge palaces, and sadly he talked of the men who would never return.

The people of Cornwall listened and wept.

And when he was alone again, in the quiet of his tiny bedroom, his thoughts drifted back to the strange fortune-teller whose words had given him the courage to attempt his escape. After twenty-three long years of captivity Thomas Pellow had found his way home.

Children's story books like this one, made possible by the support of Sanlam, are long overdue; for children of all races in this country need their immediate reality recreated for them.

True enough, some children's literature in English has been coming off the presses in a steady stream, texts that the readers can tune into, identify with. But these more recent publications differ from stories like "Little Red Riding Hood" and other Grimm's fairy tales, or *Alice in Wonderland*. As growing children, many of us found these tales enchanting, even those descended from a traditional African past, whose folklore recreated a different magic world populated by spirits who commanded a different extended metaphor.

I am aware, also, that a child's imagination is readily intrigued by any world beyond that of his own concrete reality, as long as the language allows access to the essence of this supernatural reality and the narrative is entertaining.

Yet the time has come that we should replay the child's contemporary life-drama with which he or she is most familiar. The stories in this collection do just that, in a variety of ways. The child is given a close-up picture of familiar people, things and events. Wonder time, magic time, mystery time: these are what the tales invite the child to experience. A cross-section of multicultural contributions has been achieved through the choice of writers and material which, in itself, reminds us that we should be working towards a common metaphor, just as we should arrive at a common public morality through other disciplines.

Even the snatches of folklore in the book – "Rabbit and Lion", "The frog who wanted to be red", "Mpipidi and the motlopi tree", "The singing dog" and "Kakhuni in the Valley of Lasting Dew" – all these are retold in a modern idiom that conjures up contemporary times. There is in them an immediacy that lifts them from the "Once-upon-a-time" mode, a mode that inevitably accentuates the element of improbability.

Here, then, we have an entertaining volume of stories that taps the child's world of real, familiar phenomena and of fantasy: a world of balloons, baby mice, rabbits, lions, classrooms, rubbish bins, a market, myna birds, a sausage dog, neon lions, frogs, dreams, a magic stick, milk goats, mines, a robot, crystals. And the reader, riding on the same wavelength in thought and feeling, can identify with the little boy who cries, in innocent wonder: "I like volcanoes. They can spit fire."

That the stories are intended to be read aloud enhances the value of the collection. The average reading time is just right for the child's attention span. And the stories are eminently suitable for children to practise reading aloud and silently, as well as for dramatization in class. Small groups of pupils can work out dialogue and action and see which of them are best at creating a play.

The collection is also ideal for parents to share with their children at home.

Congratulations to the compilers and editor on a book that is at once entertaining and an aesthetic delight.

Stories
South of the Sun

READ-ALOUD STORIES
COMPILED BY
CHRISTEL AND HANS BODENSTEIN
AND LINDA RODE

TAFELBERG

The publication of *Stories South of the Sun* has
been made possible by a generous book donation by Sanlam
to the READ Educational Trust during Sanlam's
seventy-fifth anniversary in 1993.

''Kakhuni in the Valley of Lasting Dew'' by Kasiya Makaka
originally appeared in *The old man of the waterfalls*,
Tafelberg Publishers, 1992;
''Rabbit and Lion'' by Hugh Tracey originally appeared in
The Lion on the Path, Routledge & Paul, 1967.

Stories originally written in Afrikaans
have been translated into English by Dianne Hofmeyr
and Hans Bodenstein.

The stories were tried out with children by
Connie Molefakgotla of Nkholi School, Sophie Moche and
Jackie Lentle of Molaetsa School in Soweto, and Jane Katane
of Kroondal Farm School in the Rustenburg district.

Final editor Annari van der Merwe.
Design and typography by Linda Rademeyer.
Illustrations by Elizabeth Andrew, Alida Bothma,
Cora Coetzee, Nikki Jones, Vusi Malindi, Terry Milne,
Zwelethu Mthethwa, Joan Rankin,
Brandan Reynolds, Mel Todd and Ann Walton.
Cover drawing by Zwelethu Mthethwa.
Set in 12 on 14 pt. Photina
by National Book Printers, Goodwood, Cape.
Printed by Toppan Printing Company (H.K.) Limited,
Hong Kong.
First edition, second impression 1996.

ISBN 0 624 02616 7

Contents

DIANNE HOFMEYR
The yellow balloon

ILLUSTRATED BY ALIDA BOTHMA

IT IS SO QUIET. The streetlights are still shining but the stars are pale against the silver sky.

"Poppie," Mama whispers, "why are you awake so early?" But before Poppie can answer, Mama smiles and nods. "I know," she says. "Today is the day of the school picnic!"

Outside in the street, people are beginning to hurry to work. Poppie's heart sings. Today she too must hurry.

But look! An empty bus is rattling down the street. Now another. One, two, three . . . and still they come. Too many to count.

"Hurry, hurry, Poppie! It's the picnic buses!" calls Mama. "Are you ready? Be careful at the lake! Go well!"

The children call out greetings as they rush to climb on the buses.

"Dumela!"

There's Thoko, Poppie's best friend. "Hello, Thoko!"

"Kunjani! Kunjani! Poppie!"

Now the buses leave . . .

"Over the bumps, past the dumps!"

"Under the bridges. Over the ridges."

"Up and down. Through the town."

"Robots are flashing! Cars are dashing!"

"In and out! Too many to count!"

"Toyota! Toyota!"

"I saw it first."

"That's my Citi Golf!"

"Coke adds life . . . that one's mine!"

Shu! At last! The buses stop in the shade of some trees. Now the parking place is crammed full, like a tin packed with fish.

There are so many buses. There are so many children. There are so many trees. And the sky looks like a big blue cloth.

"It's picnic time!" the teachers call out.

"Cooldrinks! Hot, hot hot-dogs! Cold, cold cold-dogs! Simba, Simba, Simba chips! Sweets! Sweets! Lick your lips!"

But listen . . . here comes the band. Trumpets and trombones flash. Drumsticks twirl. Cymbals crash. Drum majorettes march and legs kick high.

"Come on, Poppie! Hurry up, Thoko! It's time for marching!"

"Chucka . . . chucka . . . chuck!
Cha . . . cha . . . choo!
Schucka . . . lucka . . . luck!
Bana . . . bana . . . boo!
Bana basekolo . . . children of the school."

But now Poppie and Thoko are tired of marching. They twirl and whirl until the trees swirl around their heads like flying birds. And they somersault until the sky lies in the lake and the lake lies in the sky.

"Look at me! Look at me!" Poppie rolls and rolls until the grass wraps around her like a green rug.

Ah! Here comes the man with the machine for pumping up balloons. There are so many balloons. Everyone reaches up and pulls for a string.

"I want blue!"

"Green for me!"

"Pink! Pink! Pink!"

"Purple!"

"Orange!"

"Red is best!"

And Poppie gets a yellow one.

"Oh, look! The balloons have words on them! Read the words!"

"Mine says . . . PARTY TIME!"

"Mine says . . . 1, 2, 3 – NOW CATCH ME!"

"IT'S TRUE – I'M BLUE!"

"SMILE A WHILE!"

And Poppie reads: "KEEP BRIGHT – DON'T FIGHT!" on her yellow balloon.

"Come! We're going to send the words up into the sky! All together now . . . one, two, three . . . Let go! Everybody let go your balloons!"

But Poppie holds tight for a moment longer.

"Let go, Poppie!" Thoko shouts.

It's almost too late. Will her yellow balloon catch the others? It chases after them. But wait! What's happening?

"Oh, no! Poppie's balloon is stuck!"

"It's caught in the tree!"

"It's going to pop!"

Poppie squeezes her eyes tight shut and covers her ears.

"No, there it goes again."

The whole sky is full of balloons . . . blue, green, pink, purple, orange, red and yellow.

"Smarties! They look like Smarties in the sky!"

"If they fall down, we can eat them."

"You can't eat balloons," says Poppie. "They pop inside you and get stuck."

The balloons float up and up and up. They get smaller and smaller. Poppie can no longer read the words KEEP BRIGHT – DON'T FIGHT on her balloon. Where is her message going? She watches and watches until she sees only a small yellow dot far, far away.

Now the trees draw long, thin shadows across the grass. The sun is low. It's time to pack up. They wait in long queues, first for the toilets and then for the buses.

On the way home everyone is very quiet. They are too tired to play. Poppie rests her head on Thoko's shoulder and thinks of the many balloons floating so high up across the sky.

Who will find her yellow balloon and read the message?

When the bus stops, there is Mama waiting outside the school with all the other mothers. But look! Mama wears a dress blue like the colour of the sky. And Mama's dress is full of dots . . . green, pink, purple, orange and red. And look! There, bigger than the other dots, is a yellow one that looks just like Poppie's yellow balloon in the sky.

"Hello, Mama!"

"Hello, Poppie!"

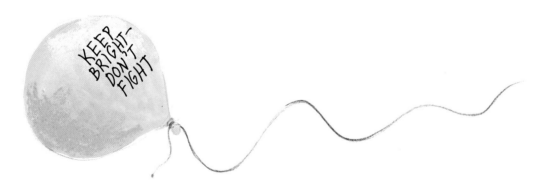

AVRIL VAN DER MERWE
Robert's rotten week

ILLUSTRATED BY JOAN RANKIN

ON MONDAY ROBERT's class did painting. Robert loved painting, especially when he could mix his own colours. He mixed red and blue together and made purple. He mixed red and yellow together and made orange. And he mixed yellow and blue together and made green.

Then Robert mixed red and blue and yellow and purple and orange and green together, and made . . . brown. Robert was very pleased with his brown paint. It reminded him of mud. He smeared it all over his page with both hands. He drew lines in it with his fingers.

He flicked it with his fingers and made interesting little mud-coloured dots all over the table, his jeans, his T-shirt, his hair and the classroom wall. He added water to it to make it thinner. A little too much water, because he actually made a muddy brown paint river that ran across the table and turned into a muddy brown paint waterfall that poured over the side of the table to make a muddy brown paint pool on the floor.

Megan walked through the pool by mistake, and made muddy brown paint footprints all the way up to Mrs Kimble.

Monday *would* have been a good day at school, except . . . Mrs Kimble did not like Robert's muddy brown paint river, or his waterfall or his pool on the floor, or the footprints. She turned an odd shade of pink, and said in a very quiet, strange-sounding voice: "Robert, clean up that mess at once!"

I wonder how you make pink, thought Robert, but he did as he was told, and it took

ages, especially as his painting paper was stuck to the table.

On Tuesday Robert's class did Show and Tell.

He had brought his white mouse and her ten babies to school to show, and to tell how he had watched the baby mice being born. He was so excited, he could hardly wait for his turn.

At last he stood proudly in front of the class, beside the teacher, and carefully took Nancy, the mother mouse, out of her cage to hold up for everyone to see. It was a little awkward trying to hold Nancy in one hand and her cage in the other, and Robert did not quite manage to get the cage door shut properly, but he didn't think it would matter much.

Only it did – because in the middle of explaining how the baby mice were born, one of the babies popped out of the cage, ran down Robert's leg and across the mat where the children were sitting.

Robert quickly gave Nancy to Mrs Kimble to hold, but Nancy did not like to be given away so suddenly, and she bit Mrs Kimble on the finger. Mrs Kimble screamed and dropped Nancy. Robert got a fright and dropped the cage. And Nancy and her babies scampered across the floor in different directions, with all the children shrieking and chasing after them.

Miss Pinney, the principal, came to see what all the rumpus was about. She calmed down Mrs Kimble and the children and helped Robert catch his mice.

9

Tuesday *would* have been a good day at school, except . . . Mrs Kimble did not seem to like Robert's mice. Her face turned a deep orange, and she said: "Robert, don't you ever bring those creatures to school again!" in a not-so-soft voice, with the words sort of squeezing themselves out from between her teeth.

Robert took his mice home, and practised saying things through his teeth, like "I've had enough to eat, thank you." It had a sort of buzzing sound, a bit like a washing machine. His mother thought he was coming down with something, so she gave him some ghastly green medicine and sent him to bed early.

On Wednesday Robert was a "helper". So were Chris and Phillip and Jessica and Robyn. They had to tidy the classroom after art, and set the tables for snack-time. Robert had been looking forward to snack-time, because it was Samantha's birthday, and she had brought a huge cake with all sorts of delicious-looking decorations on it.

At last it was time. The five children spread the tablecloths neatly over the tables and put a vase of flowers in the middle of each. Then Chris, Phillip, Jessica and Robyn went to join the others to wash their hands before eating.

Robert stayed behind and looked thoughtfully at the tables. Perhaps he should put the cake on one of the tables too. Now where was it? Oh yes, on top of Mrs Kimble's cupboard. He couldn't reach it. So he dragged a chair over to stand on.

Robert leaned across the top of the cupboard as far as he could and grabbed hold of the cake plate. The chair squeaked and slipped from under his feet. He tried to get his balance back, but . . . The chair fell over, Robert fell over, the cake fell over, with Robert's face in it – just as Mrs Kimble walked in!

Wednesday *would* have been a good day at school, except . . . Samantha was rather upset about her cake, and just wouldn't stop wailing. And Mrs Kimble was upset about

Samantha's cake, and her face seemed to swell up and get very red. Pointing at the classroom door, she yelled: "Robert! Out!"

Robert stood outside the classroom licking as much of the icing off his face as he could, wondering why Mrs Kimble had suddenly reminded him of a toffee apple.

On Thursday Mrs Kimble seemed to have forgotten how upset she had been because of Robert, and she smiled quite pleasantly at him when he said: "Good morning." Later, when he asked her for some paper to make a paper jet, she kindly said that he could use the computer paper. Some of the other boys wanted to make paper jets too.

Robert knew which was the computer paper, because Mrs Kimble had often handed out separate sheets of it to draw on. Robert *didn't* know that computer paper was all stuck together, and that each sheet had to be torn off at the perforations. So he was very surprised when, walking across the classroom with his sheet of paper, he heard the other boys giggling. He turned around to see that he was being followed by a whole trail of paper!

He jerked it to tear off a piece, but that just made things worse. The other boys jumped on it, but it tore off in the wrong places, so that Robert had to keep going back for more. It was a joke! They jumped over it and on it, and threw it at each other, watching it unravel in waves of white folds. They scrunched up some of the torn fragments and sent little balls flying through the air.

Thursday *would* have been a good day at school, except . . . Mrs Kimble was very angry about the paper. She looked blown up, like a balloon, and her face went purple and she kept saying: "I am very angry about this!" over and over, like a dizzy parrot.

Robert tried his best to put all the paper neatly together again, but somehow it still looked a mess, and Mrs Kimble was still saying: "I am very angry about this!" – which

made him nervous and put him off his job. So every time she said it, Robert said: "I'm very sorry about this." But that just seemed to make her more angry.

On Friday Robert was very pleased with himself. It was going to be a good end to a difficult week – he could just feel it. Nothing had gone wrong all day, and it was nearly home-time.

Mrs Kimble called the children inside. "Class," she said, "it is our turn to pack away the outside equipment. Please do it quickly and quietly."

Robert skipped outside to the road-track. He would put the go-carts away. It was his favourite job. A bit difficult to move a go-cart by yourself, but if you bent over it like this, and pushed . . . there!

It went rolling along nicely, faster and faster and faster until Robert was running, doubled over the go-cart.

Suddenly there was a squeal, and Mrs Kimble landed with a thud on her back in the go-cart, her astonished face looking up into Robert's.

Robert was very surprised to see her there.

Robert gazed at Mrs Kimble in fascination. Her face turned pink, then orange, then red, then purple . . . it started to swell up before his eyes, bigger and bigger . . . now it was a dark, dark purple . . .

Robert didn't wait to see any more. He turned and ran. Out of the school gate, down the road, across the park. He was at his own street corner when he heard . . . a loud explosion!

Friday *would* have been a good day at school, except . . . well . . . it wasn't really his fault Mrs Kimble had to go to hospital, was it?

Miss Pinney didn't seem too clear on that point when she phoned to check whether Robert had arrived home safely. But she sounded quite friendly on the phone, not cross at all, and she did say: "Goodbye, Robert, have a good weekend!"

And he *did*!

HUGH TRACEY
Rabbit and Lion

ILLUSTRATED BY CORA COETZEE

ONCE UPON A TIME, Lion was walking through the country when suddenly something small dashed out from under the bushes beside him, and Lion, without thinking, pounced on it with one paw. When he lifted up his paw, there underneath was a rabbit. Flat!

"Well . . ." said Lion, "it's a pity to waste a good rabbit." So he ate him all up.

Now when that rabbit's cousin got to hear about it, he was very angry indeed.

"This is serious," said Rabbit. "We must do something about this. Lion might develop a taste for rabbits."

He was sitting outside his hut, mumbling to himself, and eating some honey he had collected from the hills. When he looked up, there . . . in front of him . . . on the other side of the yard . . . was Li-on!

Rabbit didn't know what to do – to run away, or to stay quite still. But Lion had seen him and said:

"Good morning, Rabbit."

"Good morning, Lion."

"What have you got there, Rabbit?"

"Oh, honey . . . just honey, Lion."

"I'd like to taste some of your honey, Rabbit."

"Yes . . . certainly, Lion, c-c-certainly . . . Have all of it."

"Oh no! Just a taste, Rabbit, just a taste."

So Lion put one paw into the pot of honey and took a taste.

"Hmm-mm . . . very good honey, Rabbit. Mmm-mm, very good! Where did you get it?"

"Er . . . up in the hills, Lion, up in the hills."

"Good!" said Lion. "I'd like to collect some of that honey myself. Would you show me the way, Rabbit?"

"Er . . . yes, certainly, Lion, certainly."

"Well, you lead the way, Rabbit," said Lion.

"No-no-no-no, you lead the way, Lion. I like to see you in front, Lion," said Rabbit, remembering his poor cousin.

So on they went, and on they went, and on they went – Rabbit telling Lion which way to go, but always from behind.

"This way, Lion. That way, Lion. Up the valley, Lion. Round these trees, Lion. Straight ahead, Lion," and so on.

And then, when they had come all the way up the valley, to the foot of the steep hill where Rabbit had collected the honey, Rabbit had an idea.

"Lion," he said, "this is the place, Lion, but . . . but . . ."

"But what, Rabbit?"

"You know, Lion, this hill is far too steep for you to climb. I tell you what! You stay down here and I'll go up and throw down the honey to you."

"Good idea," said Lion.

"But Lion, how shall I know you're standing in the right place when I throw down the honey? Ah! I know. Wait a bit . . . I'll show you what to do."

Rabbit went off into the bushes with his little axe and cut himself five wooden pegs.

"Here we are, Lion! Now if you stand here, just here, with your legs stretched out like this, I'll peg each foot down in its place, so

13

that you can be sure you're on exactly the right spot."

"Good idea," said Lion.

So Rabbit pegged down all four feet for Lion.

"First this one, Lion." Bang-bang-bang! Gwe-gwe-gwe!

"Now the other one, Lion." Bang-bang-bang! Gwe-gwe-gwe!

"Now your back foot, Lion, right here." Bang-bang-bang! Gwe-gwe-gwe!

"Now the other one, Lion." Bang-bang-bang! Gwe-gwe-gwe!

And then Rabbit said: "Ah-ha? How can we be sure you're facing the right way, Lion? Oh, I know! I'll peg your tail straight out behind you, then you'll know you're looking straight ahead."

"Good idea," said Lion.

So Rabbit pegged out Lion's tail. Then he quickly ran up the steep hill, not to the nest of honey, but right to the top where there was a large boulder.

He called down: "Lion! Lion! Are you ready, Lion?"

"Yes, Rabbit."

"Mouth wide open, Lion?"

"Yes, Rabbit."

"Eyes tight shut, Lion?"

"Yes, Rabbit."

"Right-ho! Here comes the honey, Lion!"

And do you know what he did? He put his shoulder to the large boulder, and over it went, down, down the hill. BRRRM-BOOM-WHURRA-WHURRA-BOOM-BOO-OO-MMM!

Flat! Flat! It squashed Lion flat.

Then Rabbit shouted: "Hooray! Hooray! I've caught the lion who killed my cousin!"

He ran down the hill as fast as he could go, took his little knife out of his belt, and scooped Lion right out of his skin. Then he rolled up Lion's skin, put it on top of his head, and marched off home. There he pegged it out in the shade to dry. And when it was quite ready, he put it down on the floor of his hut for all the little rabbits to walk on.

And that was the end of that story.

INGRID MENNEN

Long sleeves for Mabel

ILLUSTRATED BY TERRY MILNE

IN WINTER Mabel's classmates all wore long-sleeved shirts to school. But not Mabel. She wore a puff-sleeved blouse with a round collar that her mother had made for her.

Her mother said she had to make do with it. "When Rob's shirt is too small for him, then he'll hand it down to you."

But it looked as if Rob had stopped growing.

Every morning when the class sat on the mat with their readers, Mabel noticed the white cuffs that stuck out from Nicola's jersey. And Nicola's collar was like all the others: stiff and sharp-pointed just like her father's Sunday shirt!

Nicola's mother bought Nicola's shirts at the shop. Sometimes even three at a time. Nicola had told Mabel.

Only when Mabel was reading or doing sums could she forget about her home-made blouse. For reading she got gold stars on her forehead, and her sums were always right. Her teacher often showed her work to the rest of the class. "Wow!" the children said.

The bell rang. Playtime!

Mabel and Nicola and Esti and the others started playing their favourite game. They drew a big square in the sand with a blue-gum stick; they divided the square into halves and then divided these into halves again. One of them – the keeper – stood on the middle line. This was the den and everyone else had to dash along the lines to try and take over the den. If someone managed to put her foot into the den, without being caught by the keeper, it was that person's turn to keep den.

They dashed backwards and forwards and up and down. Mabel was in the den. She was as quick as a squirrel. It was hard to catch her out. Eventually Esti managed. Mabel was pleased. Guarding the den made her hot and tired. Everyone took off their jerseys. All . . . except Mabel. Even though she was so hot that her face was blood-red.

Back in the classroom, Nicola saw Mabel's red face and her cheeks like ripe tomatoes. She leant towards Mabel. "I know why you never take your jersey off," she whispered softly.

Mabel felt her face becoming even redder. She said nothing. But Nicola's words kept tapping in her head.

The next morning after breakfast, Mabel took two handkerchiefs from her father's wardrobe. She unfolded them halfway and then tucked them carefully under the cuffs of her jersey sleeves. Now she had a narrow white rim of handkerchief sticking out from each sleeve. She went to the mirror and looked hard. Yes, they were exactly like the white cuffs of a long-sleeved shirt. They now looked just like those of Robby and Nicola and all the others.

When they were sitting on the mat at school, Mabel whispered to Nicola: "Look at my shirt! A long-sleeved one! It's new!"

But Nicola just stared at the round collar of Mabel's blouse. "You're fibbing!" she whispered.

"I'm not!" said Mabel very quickly, but her heart beat fast and she felt sick.

At playtime she sat alone under the blue-gum tree.

After school she walked home all alone.

The fib stayed with her. She felt tired and much too hot with her jersey on.

Nicola was waiting on the pavement a little way in front of her.

"Mabel," she called, "Mabel . . ."

But Mabel went on walking. She didn't want to hear.

That night, she couldn't sleep.

She lay and listened to Rob breathing in his sleep. She wished she could change places with him. Then she slowly got out of bed and went into the sitting room where her mother sat sewing in the light of the lamp.

"I don't want to go to school tomorrow," she said. "Not tomorrow and never again!"

She cried and cried until the fib and the handkerchief cuffs and the round-collared blouse were washed clean away. Little by little between sobs she told her mother everything. Her mother held her tight until she stopped crying.

The next morning Nicola was waiting at the school gate. "The others want to know if you'll play with us today," she told Mabel. "It's no fun without you."

When Mabel looked up, the first thing she saw was Nicola's friendly brown eyes. Then she saw Nicola's smile. And then she saw the round collar of the blouse that Nicola had on . . .

Then, even before they ran off to play, both girls took off their jerseys.

DH

17

E KOTZE
The gold-diggers

ILLUSTRATED BY ANN WALTON

HERMIE WAS GIVEN a helmet as a present. It looked like the kind of hard-hat that miners wear underground. He plonked it on top of his ruffled blond hair and ran off to show it to Sammy and Sally. They were visiting Grandma Kate and Grandpa Joe on the farm where Hermie lived.

"Just look at Hermie!" Sally exclaimed when she saw him. She and Sammy were sitting at the water furrow with bamboo sticks and lines with bent pins. "We're catching frogs," Sammy said. They looked at Hermie's helmet. If he turned it upside down, it would make just the right thing to put frogs in.

But Hermie had another plan for the helmet. "I'm going to use it in my mine. I'm going to look for gold." There had to be gold on the farm, and he even knew where: in the krans above the bluegum plantation behind Grandma Kate's house. Gold was exactly the same colour as the stripes in those rocks. At the foot of the krans was a gravel pit. That was a good place to start digging. "If I find gold, I'll be rich, and I'll be able to buy just what I want." He shut his eyes tightly to think about it.

He wanted a penknife and a tree-house; a spacesuit and a Brave Star suit and a Spiderman suit; a helicopter with batteries, and a mountain bike with four wheels as well. "You can both help me dig, then we'll share the gold," he said.

Sammy and Sally put their fishing rods down and they fetched a pick and spade from the shed. Hermie was the mine captain. He walked in front with the helmet on his head and the pick over his shoulder. Sammy carried the spade and Sally carried a bag of ripe peaches.

"Good grief, you look like three pack-horses," Grandpa Joe exclaimed as he came by with a wheelbarrow-load of pumpkins.

"No, we're miners. We're going to dig for gold," Hermie said.

"So you're going prospecting," Grandpa Joe laughed. "Well, watch out for things that sting!"

"We're going pro-spect-ing, pro-spect-ing, pro-spect-ing," they sang as they marched on.

"Well, mind how you eat those peaches," Grandma Kate called out from the washplace at the water furrow. "Watch out for stains on your clothes! Why don't you rather chop wood so that I can stoke the fire in the oven? I need to bake bread."

"No, Grandma, we're going pro-spect-ing," Hermie called out over his shoulder. "If we find gold, we'll buy you an electric oven," and they ran on.

On one side of the gravel pit was a bank of yellow clay. When it rained they used to dig it out and make animals with it. The soft clay was a good place to start. Mine tunnels were long and deep. Their tunnel would run underneath the bluegum plantation and underneath the orchard and past Hermie's house! They began to dig, but it was summer and the ground was hard.

"We'll have to make another plan," Hermie said. "Sally, fetch some water so that we can wet the ground."

There was a bucket with a wire handle

near the pigsty. Sally used it to fetch water from the spring. The path to the spring was steep, and she struggled back and forth, spilling water all the way.

It was hard work. They dug and dug and dug and Sally fetched water. It went on for the whole morning. Every time a few clods broke loose, they checked to see if there wasn't any gold yet. Perhaps they would dig open a reef and find a bank of gold lying there. Then they'd have thousands of rands, even a million or maybe a thousand million! They'd be unbelievably rich! "I'll buy a real helicopter, or an aeroplane, or a spaceship to fly around the world or even to the moon!" Hermie said.

They were so busy, they didn't hear the lunch-time whistle or the other farm noises of the tractors and lorries. It was past noon but the sun was still fierce. They sweated in the heat. It baked down in the gravel pit. It baked on Hermie's helmet. His head seemed to bake as well. He took the helmet off and hung it on a bush and took his shirt off too. Then Sammy took *his* shirt off, as well as his shoes and socks. The gnats and horseflies worried them and Sally waved them away and swatted them.

Later Sammy wiped his face with his cloth hat, rested on his spade and sighed. He looked at the shade of the trees and at the hole in the clay wall . . . and he dropped the spade with a clang. "No, there's no gold here," he said. "Grandpa Joe would've known if there was."

Hermie saw that Sammy wasn't going to dig any further. He said boldly: "Ha! What does Grandpa Joe know?"

"He knows everything," Sammy said.

"He knows nothing about gold," Hermie said. "Not a thing!"

They almost started to fight.

Sammy picked up his shirt and Hermie shouted at him: "Well, go then, but remember you'll get nothing. The gold's all mine and Sally's. Come on, Sally, *you* dig a bit," he said, and held out the spade to her.

But chink! the bucket clattered out of Sally's hand. "I'm not playing any more either. I'm too hungry." And she ran after Sammy.

"Sis! Then you can't ride in my helicopter or play in my tree-house. You're not my friends!" Hermie shouted.

"We don't want to be!" they shouted back.

Hermie dug for a while longer but he was hungry too. It was no fun being on the mountain alone. Suddenly he wasn't in the mood for digging any longer. He didn't care if there was gold or not. He didn't like dark tunnels anyway! And he wished he hadn't shouted at Sammy and Sally. He wished they were all eating Grandma Kate's honey-bread. He felt like calling after them, but he was still half-cross and half-ashamed.

Dragging his feet, he walked through the bluegum trees. He should've remembered to put on his shoes. Suddenly he felt a sharp pain in his leg. He bent down to smear some spit on the sore place and saw two scratches above his ankle. It must be a snake! "Help, help!" he shouted as loudly as he could, and clutched his leg tightly. He called for his mother and father even though he knew they'd gone to the market, and he called for Grandma Kate and Grandpa Joe.

Sammy and Sally came running through the bluegum trees. Their eyes opened wide when they saw the two identical scratch marks.

Sammy knew about tourniquets because his father worked for the Metro Emergency Service in the Cape. He tied his hanky very tightly round Hermie's leg above the bite marks. Hermie felt tears coming. He pulled a face. His leg was burning and sore. "Go and fetch Grandpa Joe, please!"

Sally ran off like a rabbit. "Help!" she shouted. "Snake!"

"Will I die, Sammy?" Hermie asked. "Look how purple my foot is. Look at the swelling."

Sammy gave the hanky one more twist. "Perhaps it wasn't such a poisonous snake. Perhaps it'll help if you put your foot in some water."

Sammy wanted to piggy-back Hermie, but he couldn't manage. Hermie was much bigger and heavier. He put his arm around Sammy's shoulder and they struggled down to the water furrow. He sank down onto the ground. The pain was worse and his foot seemed even bluer. "Sammy, if I die, you can have my miner's hat. You're my best friend. You can be mine captain. And Grandpa Joe . . ."

"Here I am." Grandpa Joe was suddenly there next to them. "What's this I hear about a snake?" He looked at the tourniquet and Hermie's swollen foot and he inspected the scratch marks carefully.

Then he untied the hanky.

"It's no wonder your foot is swollen. You tied the thing far too tight. Luckily, it's not a snakebite – it's just a thorn scratch – otherwise there'd have been trouble, because your parents have gone to town and Grandma Kate has gone to collect wood. When they get home there'll be trouble in any case, if they see how dirty you all are. Go and wash and put your shirts back on and put the tools away. It's late already."

Hermie felt his foot cautiously, and then he limped after Sally and Sammy.

Later, when the sun was setting, they sat washed and clean in front of Grandma Kate's house, eating thick slices of fresh honey-bread. The yellow krans had turned brown and was full of shadows. The moon came up and hung over the rocks so that its edge just touched the highest point.

"Ahh!" sighed Hermie. "Look how close it seems. I'd like to climb up there and get it down."

But Sammy shook his head beneath Hermie's miner's helmet. "I wouldn't!" he said.

"Nor me," said Sally. "Tomorrow we're going to buy a real line and hook and catch frogs."

DH

JAY HEALE
Boo Brat Bangles

ILLUSTRATED BY NIKKI JONES

BRAT IS MY LITTLE BROTHER. He was called Brian once, but not any more. His favourite game is hide-and-seek. It drives us all mad, because Brat only does the hiding part: Mum goes to put away the ironing and – BOO! goes Brat, jumping out of the linen cupboard. Dad starts to mow the lawn and – BOO! goes Brat, landing on him out of the tree. Our dachshund was so scared she used to hide under the bed. She doesn't do that any more. Brat hides there first. BOO! goes Brat, and the poor dog's a nervous wreck.

He does it to me too, but since I've started hitting him with the nearest thing I can grab, he doesn't do it so much. My doll has a harder head than he has!

I used to escape Brat for half the day when I went to school. I like school. I'm in Standard one. It's fun there. Helen, that's my best friend, sits next to me and she's the greatest giggler you've ever known.

But the playschool threw Brat out and said it was time he "went up". So he came to terrorise Sub A. He was known as "Boo Brat" before he'd been there a week.

There are all sorts of interesting kids at our school now. Zuko runs faster than anyone, even Brat. He speaks Xhosa *and* English. Fatima has the prettiest long black hair. She's Malay. Helen and I weren't sure about being friends with Fatima at first. She was so shy and only spoke in a whisper.

Then Mum invited all the class home for my birthday and that was when we first saw Fatima's bracelets. She has loads of them! Silver and copper and some with tiny beads in bright colours. She can't wear them at school, of course. Not with a school uniform. But in her party dress with these bracelets on each wrist she looked beautiful.

So Helen and I sat down with Fatima on the settee, turning her bangles round and round, and soon she was showing us how to plait our hair. That's when it happened . . . BOO! goes Brat, leaping out from behind the curtains. Fatima screamed. Helen gasped. I hit him with a cushion. Brat laughed and said: "Oh, look! Bangles!"

Poor Fatima! When Brat jumped out on most kids, it was just BOO! But from then on, when he spotted Fatima, it was BOO BANGLES! – and yells of laughter as Fatima screamed.

"You've got to stand up to him," we told her.

She shook her long black plaits. "I'm too scared," she whispered.

We tried everything to stop Brat's Boo-game. We yelled at him. We ganged up on him. Zuko chased him round the playground. Brat just grinned and found some more places to hide. The tuck-shop lady goes to the big cardboard box of chips and – BOO! goes Brat, and the chips fly everywhere. The art teacher piles up the trays of paint and – BOO! goes Brat from under the table, and there's paint sloshing all over the floor.

"I'm sorry, Miss," I said, for what seemed the hundredth time. "I know he's my brother, but I wish he wasn't. I wish he'd hide somewhere and get lost!"

Perhaps that's what gave Fatima the idea.

22

She never said anything at the time. She just looked more nervous every day, and she told Helen that she wasn't enjoying our school much. It was all my brother's fault, she said. Helen told me and I told Brat and he didn't seem to care.

"It's only a game. Boo Bangles doesn't really mind much."

"Brat – she *does*."

He shrugged. I hate my brother when he shrugs.

Next day he jumped her again. Fatima was

on her way across the parking area after Assembly when – BOO BANGLES! goes Brat from behind the school bus. Fatima didn't scream. She just ran away!

Brat was laughing so much he didn't see which way she went.

That's what he told Miss when she sent for him.

"Now we don't know where Fatima is," Miss said. "She never came to class. What can you tell us?"

Brat looked a little nervous, for the first time ever. He didn't like being sent for by Miss. "I . . . I don't know," he stammered. "I played a joke on her and she ran away."

Miss looked at him sternly. "They say you're very fond of hiding. It's time you did some seeking as well. Go and find Fatima."

So Brat began to search. There weren't all that many places in our school where you could hide for long. Brat knew all of them. The classrooms, the cupboards, the bike sheds, the cloakrooms.

He stopped outside the girls' toilets, embarrassed. Helen and I searched those for him. Fatima wasn't there. We knew that. We'd looked there long ago.

"It's all your fault!" hissed Helen. "She could have run outside and got murdered or run over."

"She wouldn't do that. She's too scared," Brat muttered.

Actually, we were fairly sure that Fatima had not left school, because they lock the gates during the morning and the groundsman sits in his little box with the key.

"Then where is she, Brat?" I asked.

"I don't know." He was worried now.

He went on searching. Everyone knew what was happening.

"Come on, Boo Brat!" they called.

"You're 'Bang' Brat now!" said one of the boys. "You're frightened."

And Brat *was* frightened.

He searched the school buildings, the playing fields, the car park. That only left the unpleasant place round the back where the rubbish goes. Brat didn't like it there. But we were all following him, and Miss, and some of the other teachers too. He peered under the tin roof, into the dark shadows full of smells and nastiness.

"Go on," said Zuko.

"I don't want to," said Brat.

"You have to," we all said.

That was when it happened.

In amongst the smelly rubbish and tins and boxes was one shiny new steel dustbin with the lid tilted ever so slightly. As Brat went towards it, the lid flew up and clanged away.

"Boo Brat Bangles!" shrieked a voice we all knew.

And Brat burst into tears . . .

Fatima smiled shyly when all the fuss had died down. "I didn't know what to do at first," she explained. "I just wanted to run away."

"We thought you might have tried to go home," I said.

"I'm not that stupid!" said Fatima. "No. I hid in that clean new dustbin to be safe from Brat. Then I heard him looking for me and I had a better idea. I thought I'd give *him* a fright for a change!"

And that was how Fatima found her courage, the school found something else to talk about for a bit, and Brat became known as "Boo Brat Bangles" for almost ever after.

DIANNE STEWART
Market mischief

ILLUSTRATED BY MEL TODD

"TIME TO GET UP, DEVI!"

Oh, no! Devi thought. It's too early! But then she suddenly remembered it was Saturday. She loved Saturdays, because on Saturdays she helped her mother at the market.

She dressed quickly in her green checked overall, and twisted her hair into a long plait, as dark and shiny as the skin of a brinjal.

She and her mother were at the market before sunrise. Several other stall-holders were already at work, and in the surrounding trees black-and-brown myna birds chattered excitedly. Devi smiled. They too were up early, waiting to see what they could get from the market.

When the lorries arrived to deliver fruit and vegetables to the stall-holders, Devi helped carry boxes of produce into the building. She was just nearing the doorway with a box of plums in her hands when she suddenly tripped. The box slid from her hands – and splosh! The ripe purple plums fell to the ground. Soon the cheeky mynas dived down to feast on the spoils. They screeched and squawked each other out of the way as their sharp yellow beaks pecked at the scarlet flesh of the burst plums.

"What a mess!" sighed Devi in dismay, as she tried to shoo them away from the doorway with a sweep of her thin, bangled arms.

Reluctantly, the mynas took to the air, but hovered above the doorway to see if there was any chance of returning to their feast. Devi watched the birds fly into the market building through an open window.

After clearing up the mess she went inside.

The mynas were strutting around the steel girders that support the roof. "Naughty birds," Devi whispered smilingly when she saw them disturbing a sparrow which was trying to build a nest.

At seven the main doors of the market were flung open to let in the daylight and the customers.

"It's the end of the month. There will be a lot of people buying today," said Devi's mother, as she put fresh ginger into packets. "We're going to be busy."

Devi was weighing onions on a large black scale in her mother's stall. When she glanced at Mrs Naidoo's stall right next to her mother's, she saw large white and ochre-coloured pumpkins sitting in neat rows at the back of the stall. Fire-red chillis, bulbous green peppers and ripe tomatoes were neatly arranged in boxes.

Devi quickly rearranged some of the vegetables at the front of her mother's stall. She hoped to attract as many customers as Mrs Naidoo. A myna squawked from above, and when Devi looked up, it nodded its head approvingly at her arrangement.

"Pick out your own tomatoes!" Mrs Naidoo called to her customers. She did not mind if her tomatoes were prodded and poked by many fingers!

On the other side was Mr Maharaj's fruit-stall. All the children loved him as he always gave them fruit to eat. He was well known for his "honey-pot" grapes, as he called them. But Devi had read on the box that they were actually "hanepoot" grapes.

Mr Maharaj walked across to Mrs Naidoo, leaving his stall unattended. Looking up, Devi saw two mynas fly down from the girders to perch on top of Mr Maharaj's stall. They bobbed their white-tipped tails up and down and fixed their yellow-ringed eyes on his grapes.

"Quick, Mr Maharaj!" shouted Devi. "Those mynas are after your honey-pot grapes!"

She rushed over and helped Mr Maharaj chase the birds away. They flew back towards the roof, protesting noisily.

After she had weighed the onions and put them in kilogram packets, Devi said to her mother: "I'm going across to help Mrs Govender at the spice-stall. She has a long line of customers."

As Devi entered Mrs Govender's stall, she was surrounded by spicy Eastern aromas: the tangy smell of the bright red chilli powder, the marigold-yellow turmeric powder and the sweeter cinnamon smell of the garam masala.

"Hello, Devi," Mrs Govender said, "glad you've come. I need your help. What are these noisy birds doing inside our market hall?" she added in the same breath, glaring up at the mynas which were chattering right above her spice-stall. "Keep an eye on them, Devi!" she added.

Devi had just carefully measured out some turmeric powder for a customer when the chattering of the mynas changed to a high-pitched screech, accompanied by a frantic fluttering of wings. She looked up and saw the mynas harassing the sparrow again. How alike in colour the turmeric powder and the mynas' beaks and legs are, she thought, when – suddenly – there was a thud! Devi jumped back. She could not believe her eyes. There, in the chilli powder right in front of Mrs Govender, lay a half-dazed myna!

Atshoo! Atshoo! sneezed Mrs Govender. "Help! Quick! My eyes are burning . . ." Chilli powder flew in all directions. Customers in the queue ducked, laughed and sneezed. The myna got up, shook its feathers vigorously, spreading red powder everywhere. After a while it fluttered about with shut eyes, just missing Mrs Govender's face, and then flew out through the main door of the market.

Devi wiped Mrs Govender's face with a handkerchief. She looked so strange with all that red dust on her hair, tears streaming down her cheeks. But Devi could see how angry she was and so she tried hard not to laugh.

"Those myna birds will have to go!" shouted Mrs Govender. "They've ruined my spices. Out with you! Out, out, out!"

But the mynas remained sitting on the top rafters in a neat, straight line. When Devi looked up they started their concert. What she heard was: "Atshoo . . . Atshoo! Out . . . Out . . . Out!"

The next week Mrs Govender called a meeting of all the stall-holders in the market. Together they arranged for gauze to be put on all the windows in the building to keep out the mynas.

Devi felt rather sorry for the birds. She missed their antics inside the building. But the mynas did not disappear. Every Saturday she saw them strutting around the car-park next to the market building, and whenever she could, she fed them discarded fruit – which they found far more tasty than Mrs Govender's red-hot chilli powder.

KLAUS KÜHNE

The longest sausage dog in the world

ILLUSTRATED BY JOAN RANKIN

NICHOLAS WAS IN DISGRACE. He had told a lie. A fib, a whopper.

"I didn't, I didn't!" Nicholas cried. But nobody would believe him. After all, little boys do sometimes stretch the truth.

"I saw a sausage dog as long as a house!" was what Nicholas had said.

"Rubbish!" said Catherine.

"Tell me another!" said Mother.

"Nicholas!" said Father.

"I believe you," said Grandma.

"What?" exclaimed the whole family.

"I know when a boy is telling the truth," Grandma said. "Or to put it differently, when he tells exactly what he *saw*." She was knitting something fluffy and pink. The knitting needles clicked and clattered between her busy fingers. "Nicholas, now tell me what you saw."

Nicholas sniffed a couple of times. Grandma handed him a tissue. "Blow your nose first," she said.

"I saw a sausage dog . . ." Nicholas began.

"You saw a dachshund," Catherine said.

"I was standing at the front gate," Nicholas continued. "I saw . . . I saw a sausage dog peeping round the corner of the house across the road. It had a pointy brown face and a thin pointy tail like a piece of sucked liquorice."

"Trust you to think of food," Catherine said.

"Shush," said Grandma.

"He was drinking from the tap and wagging his tail."

"That doesn't make him as long as a house," said Father.

"But the tap is on one side of the house and he was wagging his tail on the *other* side of the house!" Nicholas insisted.

"Now tell me," said Grandma, "when did those people move in?"

"Yesterday," said Mother. "Yesterday morning. I took them a loaf of bread, remember?"

"And how many sausage dogs do they own?" Grandma asked.

"One," said Mother. "It barked at me."

"Well, I saw two sausage dogs barking at the milkman this morning," Grandma said quietly. "That's why I knew Nicholas was telling the truth."

"So Nicholas saw the head of one . . ."

" . . . and the tail of the other one!"

"Thank you, Grandma!" Nicholas cried. "You see, I wasn't telling a fib!"

"I could tell you weren't," said Grandma. "I once had the same experience when I was a little girl. I was accused of telling a lie and it hurt me very much."

"Grandma, you never tell lies!" Catherine cried.

"I try not to."

"What happened to you, Grandma?" Nicholas asked.

"Things were different when I was a little girl. The milk was delivered by horse and cart, and when we went on holiday, the train was pulled by a steam engine. There were very few motor cars and a ride in one was a great treat."

"That must have been a long, long time ago," said Nicholas.

"It was," said Grandma. "And the biggest treat of all was when an aeroplane flew across our town. Then we would all run outside to look at it. Today there are so many aeroplanes, we don't even bother to look up."

"But now we run outside to look at a horse," chuckled Father.

"Indeed we do," said Grandma. "Imagine, I had never seen an aeroplane on the ground. I'd only seen them high in the sky – and of course they only looked so big." Grandma held up the bedsock she was knitting.

"One morning I was playing with my dolls on the stoep when an aeroplane came flying over the fowl run! It skimmed past the fig tree, just missed the windpump and landed among the cabbages at the bottom of the garden. It was yellow and blue and it had two wings, one above the other.

"I rushed back into the house and cried: 'Come and look, come and look, an aeroplane has landed in the vegetable garden!'

"My brothers and my father and my mother came running as fast as they could. I raced down the steps to the street and . . . it was gone!

"'Where is it? Where is it?' gasped my mother.

"Her hands were all white with flour because she was baking bread that morning.

"'It was there a moment ago,' I said. 'It must have flown off again.'

"'You fibber!' my brothers roared.

"My father put his hand gently on my head. 'An aeroplane is much too big to land in the vegetable garden,' he said. 'How could you make up such a fantastic story?'

"'I did see an aeroplane land in the vegetable garden. I did!' I wailed. But nobody would believe me and I was upset for days.

"It was some weeks later that I discovered what had really happened. The boys who lived at the top of the hill had built a model aeroplane and flown it down the street!

"While I was inside the house, fetching the family, they must have picked up their toy and run away again."

Grandma paused to count her stitches. "That's why I like to think first before I call someone a liar."

"You see!" Nicholas said, glancing at the others. And then he gave Grandma a big hug.

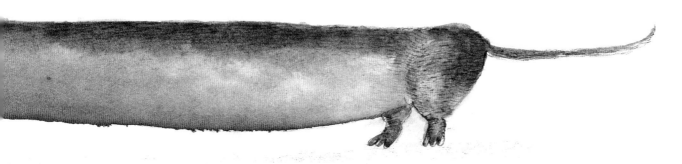

NOLA TURKINGTON
An-ki-saw-rus in Africa

ILLUSTRATED BY JOAN RANKIN

BRUCE WRAPPED HIS catapult in an old hankie. "Snedi, wait for me," he shouted, stopping to stuff the catty into the pocket of his shorts. The boys were running across a farm field to the edge of the forest on the other side.

Snedi waited for Bruce. He wanted to explore the dark Tsitsikamma forest, but he didn't want to explore by himself.

"Last night Umakhulu had a dream," Snedi said to Bruce, when he had caught up with him. "She saw a deep pool in the middle of the forest. And I want to find it." He was three years older than Bruce, and much braver.

Bruce sighed. It was no use arguing with his friend about anything his granny had told him.

It was quiet among the trees. Only the sound of wind rustling the leaves of old yellowwoods disturbed the deep silence. Or . . . was it not the wind making those sighing sounds?

"Snedi," Bruce said suddenly, "let's go home. I feel scared."

"No way!" Snedi said, and moved faster down the forest path.

Bruce had a hard job climbing over dead branches on the forest floor. Soon his red hair was wet with sweat and he wished he too was nine years old, with legs as long as Snedi's.

Suddenly Snedi stood still and Bruce bumped into him from behind. Coming towards them, dressed in a silver spacesuit, was a very strange figure. She was only about a metre tall, with a round face, black button eyes and a wide red mouth. On her bald head she wore a helmet with a pocket in front.

"Snedi, oh, Snedi . . ." Bruce began, and felt for Snedi's hand. But the strange being interrupted him.

"Have you seen Anchisaurus?" she asked in a soft voice.

"Please say that again," Snedi said. She was too small for him to feel afraid.

"An-ki-saw-rus," she sounded the word slowly.

"An-ki-saw-rus," Bruce repeated. "What's that? And who are . . ."

"Just as I thought!" the small figure exclaimed. "If you humans haven't seen Anchisaurus, that's why the poor thing is still alive." She blew out her soft, silvery cheeks. Her black eyes shone with an angry glitter, and her spacesuit sparkled and crackled as if it was on fire. "Whatever walks, crawls, creeps or climbs, sooner or later you humans will harm it!" she cried out fiercely.

Snedi dropped the sharp stone he was carrying. No bird was safe from Snedi's aim. Bruce felt scared – he thought about the catty in his pocket. But he couldn't stop himself from asking questions.

"Who are you? Where do you come from?" he asked.

"My name's Moe," she said, sounding more friendly. "In my spaceship I've travelled to Earth from a Green Moon in the Galaxy."

"Why've you come?" Bruce asked.

"To rescue Anchisaurus," Moe said. Her

glittery eyes were fixed on Snedi and Bruce. "Coming?" she asked. Then suddenly she left the path and hurried into the deeper, darker forest.

The two boys followed.

It's so dark, there's no sunlight here, Snedi thought, as he looked up into the dense leafy roof that shut out the sun. He shivered, and wished he'd brought his jersey.

"Shouldn't we rather go home?" Bruce whispered. But Snedi said: "No. Let's follow her for a while."

To Bruce it seemed they would never stop. At last the three came to a valley full of giant ferns.

BOOM, BOOM, BOOM . . . A loud sound filled the forest.

"What's that noise?" Bruce asked.

"Sounds like drums," Snedi said.

"No, it's the heart of the forest, beating," Moe said. "We are close to the dark green heart of the forest now, and because no one may look into a forest's secret heart, I'll just pop out my eyes. I always take them out when necessary. It's so easy to put them back, although I have lost a pair, once or twice. So I always carry spares." Smoothly, Moe popped out her eyes, and shut her soft eyelids. Carefully she put the eyes in the pocket of her helmet.

"Wow!" Bruce cried. And Snedi decided that none of Umakhulu's stories were as exciting as this one.

"Unluckily, you two can't pop out your eyes, so you have to shut them," Moe said. "And keep them shut. Hold my hands and I'll guide you through the heart of the forest."

After a long struggle through the giant ferns, they started moving about more easily.

"Open your eyes, we've reached the other side," Moe cried, as she popped her eyes back in.

The boys saw a placid pool of green water. Growing round the pool were ferny plants. Green reeds grew on the muddy banks. Tall tree ferns and clumps of cycads stood steaming in the hot, damp air.

"There's Anchisaurus!" Moe cried. Bruce and Snedi stared in amazement. Beside the pool was a large animal. He looked like a huge lizard. He had strong legs and arms with tough claws on his thumbs, and a great

thick tail and neck but a small head. He was munching a bunch of river reeds.

"Anki! Anki!" Moe called.

"Anchisaurus is a dinosaur!" Bruce cried. "I've seen drawings of him in the colouring book Mum bought from the Museum shop. My book says dinosaurs have been dead for a million years, Moe."

"No human before you and Snedi has ever seen a live dinosaur," Moe said. "Humans have only found dinosaur bones. Hidden close to the secret heart of the forest, Anki's family survived for millions of years. But now Anki is the last dinosaur alive."

Anchisaurus stopped eating. Slowly he moved towards Moe and the boys.

He was very friendly. He nudged Bruce and Snedi and rubbed his scaly body against their bare legs.

Moe stroked Anki's head while she hummed softly to herself. Then, still with her hand on his head, Moe led Anchisaurus and the boys back in a half-circle to the place where she and Bruce and Snedi had met.

"Snedi, look up there!" Bruce cried. Snedi looked up. Hovering above the trees he saw a shiny metal machine. Shaped like a spinning top, it had puffs of pink smoke squirting out

of its periscope. A ladder led from Moe's spaceship down to the forest floor.

"Anki and I must leave Earth at once," Moe said. "Waiting on the Green Moon is a mate for Anchisaurus. She's frantic for a friend."

"Don't go, Moe!" Bruce begged. "Won't there ever be another dinosaur on Earth?"

"One day, if humans learn to really care about animals, and about forests, and if the dinosaurs on the Green Moon have babies, maybe I'll bring you a pair of little Anchisauri," Moe said.

Clumsily, Anchisaurus, and then Moe, climbed the ladder into Moe's machine. Then, in one squirt of pink smoke, the spaceship vanished.

"Snedi, have we been dreaming?" Bruce asked.

"No," Snedi said. "But I'm sure the pool near the forest's heart is the one Umakhulu dreamt of." Then he bent down and picked something up. "Look at these." In the palm of his hand lay a pair of black button eyes.

"Moe's lost her spares!" Bruce said.

Then they rushed home along the forest path, taking care not to squash the young fern plants under their feet.

REVIVA SCHERMBRUCKER
Percy and the neon lions

ILLUSTRATED BY ALIDA BOTHMA

IT IS WINTER and night comes early. Percy the newspaper vendor stands on the traffic island in the middle of Main Road, Newlands. The wind tugs at the folded newspapers he holds, and flattens his clothes against his body. He puts a brick and some stones on the pile of newspapers. Then he dances a few steps, jumps, stamps, rocks, blowing on his fingers to keep them warm.

Peep-peep! Peep-peep! A car has pulled up at the kerb and the driver is impatient. Percy dodges between the moving traffic and pushes a newspaper through a slit at the top of the driver's window. Fingers stretch out and money drops into his cold hands. He fumbles for change. Hurry! The robot has turned green. Hoot! Peep-peep!

In the gardens of the brewery across the road a family of neon lions is resting under the trees. In between selling newspapers, Percy watches the cub jump up and down and the great lion's tail wag up, down, up, down. The lions seem pleased with the job I'm doing, Percy thinks to himself.

But the night is fierce. Gusts of wind are thrashing the trees outside the hotel, and shadows race madly along the road.

"Newspaper, over here," a woman gestures.

Percy tucks a newspaper under his arm and runs towards the hotel.

But what is this sheet of paper, suddenly flapping against his legs? He looks back at his papers on the traffic island. The stones have rolled off and the newspapers are flying away. Percy dashes back, snatching and diving this

way and that. Newspapers are sailing in the night sky, wrapping themselves around telephone wires, cartwheeling into trees, tickling buildings six stories high.

Which way should he run? Where are the missing pages? Percy sits down on the small pile of crumpled papers he has caught. His head drops to his knees. What will he tell the driver when he comes to fetch him? Will he lose all his pay?

Cars hoot, the wind races, but Percy does not look up – he is like a stone.

After a long while, he hears a steady hum. A glowing red light seeps through his fingers and shines through his closed eyelids. Has someone lit a fire? he wonders. When at last he lifts his head, the big neon lion and the cub are standing beside him, soft on their paws. The great lion's mane is so bright, it is difficult to look straight at it.

"Ah, you've come to me!" Percy whispers, reaching out with his hand towards the lions. The instant his fingers touch the neon tubes, he is caught. The lions leap into action. They streak through the streets, with Percy like a speck of nothing on the great lion's back.

Zzzzzzzip! go the neon lions, weaving through the traffic, crossing in and out of the beams of light. To keep out the cold wind, Percy buries his head in the great lion's mane, which buzzes with warmth.

"Percy! Percy!" shout the other newspaper vendors as he shoots past with the lions, and "Oh no!" as the playful cub kicks over the newspaper piles on the street corners.

But Percy hangs on. The wind bends the

33

neon tubes of the lions into zigzag wings. Effortlessly, they take off into the air. Percy laughs as flying newspapers brush past him and the neon lions zoom above the trees, bucking and swerving between the tall buildings.

But suddenly the dark mountainside appears ahead. With the sound of their heavy panting in Percy's ears, the lions veer upwards . . . up, up, up into the night sky.

Percy is borne high above the city, which glitters below him as if it were alive. Thoughts of newspapers, of his job and the money he may lose become as tiny as the pin-pricks of light below. The wind is roaring and stars are wheeling as the neon lions rocket through the skyveld.

Percy is not the least bit frightened. "Whooha!" he shouts with joy as the lions dip down to skim along the seashore, and white foam flies off the waves into his face. Together he and the lions loop the loop and miss rocky cliffs by a hair's breadth. They spin tighter circles in the air and spiral down to take a look at the ships in Table Bay Harbour and the craggy mountain they call Lion's Head.

"Let's have a look at the stone lions!" Percy shouts, and immediately they swoop down low over Rhodes Memorial, where two large stone lions guard a flight of stairs. Percy can just make out the dark shapes of deer asleep on the hillside.

The lions race tirelessly, paddling on the air. Still Percy feels no fear . . . not even when the great lion turns sharply to avoid the smoke stack of a factory, causing Percy to lose his grip on the neon mane. He is swept from the great lion's back. Down, down, down he floats through the night sky, until he lands like a small stone on the grass.

There he sits in the wind, with his head between his knees, numb with excitement.

Toot! Toot! Toot! A hooter blares.

Slowly, Percy opens his eyes. Where is he? What has happened to the lions . . .? Suddenly he knows – he is back on his very own traffic island in Main Road, Newlands. He jumps up – where are his newspapers?

Toot! Toot! It is the driver of the newspaper van who is hooting to call the newspaper vendors he has come to fetch.

The driver sees Percy's confused face. "Don't worry!" he calls out. "All over town every paper boy I've seen has lost half of his papers, and even more. Mad wind blowing tonight."

As they drive off in the van, Percy looks back. The neon lions are resting under the trees. The cub jumps up and down, and the great lion wags his tail up, down, up, down . . .

SHELLEY TRACEY

The frog who wanted to be red

ILLUSTRATED BY ZWELETHU MTHETHWA

ONCE UPON A TIME, in a big green pond between tall green reeds, there lived a little green frog with his green family and his little green friends. Life was good for the little green frog. There were many brightly coloured insects to catch, and cool lily pads to rest on.

But the frog was not happy. He didn't like his green froggy skin. He wanted to be red.

One day the little green frog felt so unhappy that he decided to leave the big green pond. "I am going to look for the Great Chameleon of the Hills," he told his friends and his family. "Then I will ask him to make me red." All the other frogs begged the little green frog to stay, but he would not listen.

So off hopped the little green frog, determined to become red. He hopped over many stones, swam through many ditches, and in between he rested on mushrooms . . . until he met a bright red caterpillar. The caterpillar was curled around a shiny dark green leaf, and her redness glowed in the sunlight. "Oh, Caterpillar," said the frog, "I wish I were as red as you. You are so beautiful. I am off to the Great Chameleon of the Hills to ask him to turn me red. Bright red, just like you."

But the bright red caterpillar did not answer. She just stared at the little green frog and hugged the shiny dark green leaf with her long red body.

So off hopped the little green frog, determined to become red. Soon he came upon a magnificent scarlet rose, standing proud and tall on her thorny stem. "Oh, Rose," said the frog, "I wish I were as red as you. You are so beautiful. I am off to the Great Chameleon of the Hills to ask him to turn me a magnificent scarlet, just like you."

But the magnificent scarlet rose did not answer, just nodded a little and swayed on her thorny stem.

So off hopped the little green frog, determined to become red. He was still travelling, looking for the Great Chameleon of the Hills, when the sun began to set. The little green frog gazed at the glowing red orb of the sun as it melted into the darkening sky. "Oh, Sun," said the frog, "I wish I were as red as you. You are so beautiful. I am off to the Great Chameleon of the Hills. I'll ask him to change my green to a glowing red, just like yours."

But the glowing red orb of the sun did not answer. Slowly, slowly it sank behind the hills.

So off went the little green frog again, hopping up the steep hillside in the gathering dusk. When at last he reached the top of the Hill of the Great Chameleon, he waited breathlessly.

The stars came out, and so did the Great Chameleon of the Hills. His eyes glowed like two moons in the darkness as he greeted the little frog. "How are you, my little green friend?" he whispered. "What can I do for you?"

The little green frog peered up at the shadowy form of the great creature, but was too overwhelmed to speak. After a while he managed to croak: "Please grant me my wish, Great One. Oh, please, make me red."

36

The Great Chameleon of the Hills rolled his eyes in the darkness. "I will grant your wish, little one," he said quietly, "but it may not make you happy."

"Oh yes, it will!" the little green frog replied eagerly. "I have always longed to be red."

"Very well," answered the Great Chameleon of the Hills. "I will grant your wish. But I will also give you an extra wish. If at any time you change your mind about being red, you can wish to be green again. But I warn you – that wish will be final. Once you are green, you can never ever become red again."

"Thank you, Great One," said the little frog, "but I do not think I will ever use that second wish."

"Then close your eyes, little one," said the Great Chameleon of the Hills. "Now keep very still."

The little green frog closed his eyes. His whole body quivered with excitement. He waited and waited, and then at last he felt his body beginning to glow. He felt warm and happy, and he fell fast asleep.

Next morning, the little frog woke up on the hilltop and looked around him. The Great Chameleon of the Hills had gone. "What a wonderful dream!" said the frog to himself. Then his eyes fell on his front legs, and he beamed with joy. "What a glorious red," he cried. "Oh, how beautiful I am! I will never need the second wish. I never want to be green again."

And so the little red frog set off homewards, watching his little red feet in front of him as he hopped along.

On the way he stopped to play with some shiny red ladybirds. He was so busy playing that he forgot about going home, and it grew darker and darker. That night he took shelter with the ladybirds under a piece of loose bark, and dreamt about himself with his bright red skin, as beautiful as a rose.

The following morning, the frog woke up very early with the ladybirds and they all went out to drink some dew. Up and down the long blades of green grass they climbed, sipping the cool moisture.

Suddenly a shadow fell over them . . .

Looking up at the sky, the frog saw a great golden hawk hovering over him. The little frog was terrified. He knew that hawks catch frogs. He clung to a stalk of grass, trying to keep completely still, but he was very frightened and his bright red legs, clamped around the green stalk, shook with fear . . . His lovely bright red skin had become a danger to him!

The hawk swooped lower and its shadow loomed larger. The frog was terrified. His little red throat ballooned in and out, in and out. All of a sudden it was very quiet. The frog closed his eyes and held his breath, waiting for the hawk to grab him.

Quickly, without realising what he was doing, the frog wished he could be green. When he opened his eyes to peep, he looked down on two green front legs clamped around a green stalk. And at that moment the hawk plunged down in a swirl of golden-brown feathers and snatched up a small red snake in its talons.

The little green frog watched in fear and pity for the snake as the hawk carried it off to its nest. The frog felt thankful to be alive, and pleased to be green once more. Perhaps I am not meant to be red, he thought. Red is really beautiful – but now I know, my green skin keeps me safe.

So off hopped the little green frog to the big green pond between the tall green reeds, to tell his green family and his little green friends about all his adventures.

GERALD MULLINS
Bring and Tell

ILLUSTRATED BY ELIZABETH ANDREW

HOW COULD HE EVER like Ladysmith? thought Alan. He had no friends, and there seemed to be nothing to do.

He had moved here with his parents from Uvongo, on the South Coast. He only now realised how much he missed the sea, the beaches, friends, fishing, the call of the gulls . . . just everything.

What made it even worse was that the Christmas holidays were over, and it was his first term at the new school.

Mrs Draper, his class teacher, was nice, but so far he had spoken little with the other children in the class. "Tomorrow," said Mrs Draper, who was large, had grey hair, wore thick glasses and laughed a lot, "we will have a Bring and Tell Day. Bring anything you like and tell us about it."

Alan could not think of anything special to bring. He wished now that his mom had let him bring along his fishing-rod and reel, or his surfboard. But she'd thought it better to leave them at his grandparents' home in Uvongo.

Coming out of class, Alan spoke to Themba, who was also new and walking alone. "I haven't got anything to bring to-morrow. Have you?" said Alan.

"Oh yes," replied Themba. "But you come from the sea. You must have something – everybody has. Just do what the Bible says – seek and you will find," he added smiling.

"Thank you for nothing," said Alan, and walked away despondently.

*

"Alan, don't throw your things on the floor. Pick them up, dear. Have you made any friends yet?" Alan's mother was always busy, and seemed to say six things at once.

"No." Alan picked up two shoes, one sock and a crumpled tie, and went to his bedroom.

Seek and you will find! What a stupid thing to say, he thought. Seek means search, but search what? I've only got two drawers here. The three big boxes of stuff I had at the old house were thrown out before the move.

"Ma, we've got a Bring and Tell at school tomorrow, what should I take?"

"No need to shout, Alan. How should I know? Please bring me your dirty shirt, dear. What about the shell that old fisherman gave you, remember?"

"Ah . . .! Thanks, Ma!"

He and his dad had been fishing off the rocks when the old man fishing nearby had asked Alan if he wanted a "sea telephone", and given him the shell. How could he have forgotten about it?

"And take that rhyme along that you and Dad made up afterwards. They're both in your bottom drawer. Read it out first, then ask the class to guess what it is."

Alan cheered up at once. He scrabbled through his drawer, found the shell, and held it to his ear. Then he read the poem again.

This was going to be fun! He couldn't wait to tell his dad.

Next day he hurried to school, but when at last his turn came, all he could see were faces staring at him, waiting for him to say something. His mouth went dry.

"Don't be shy, Alan. Show us what you have brought," said Mrs Draper.

"May I . . . May I tell a poem first, Miss, and then ask the class to guess what it is?"

"*Recite* a poem, Alan, not tell. Of course you may."

Looking first at the ceiling, then at his paper, and swallowing hard, Alan began:

"I am me and I come from the sea,
  Tumbled and rumbled and tra-la-la-lee.
  Lift me up and listen to me
  For the sound of the shore –
  For evermore."

Ten hands must have gone up. "Miss, Miss!"

"Yes." She pointed at Debbie.

40

"It's a seashell, Miss."

"Is it, Alan?" Mrs Draper asked.

In answer Alan opened his parcel and brought out his shell. He had hoped it wouldn't be easy to guess, and tried to hide his disappointment. The shell was beautiful – bigger than an orange, white and grey on the outside, and shiny green, grey and blue inside. He put it to his ear, and listened.

"Very good, Alan. And what a lovely poem! Will you tell us more about it when we have more time?"

Just then the bell rang for break.

"We will continue after break, children, and I hope we have some more rhymes."

Only two children came up to him and asked to listen to the shell, and then hurried away. Things had not gone as well as he had imagined.

When he got to the playground, Themba came up to him. "So you searched." He said it as a fact. "That was good."

"No, I . . . well, yes, I did have to look."

"Help me make up a rhyme for mine, will you?"

"Well, I . . . I'm not very good, but . . ."

Themba brought out a notebook, and soon their heads were together, and they were laughing and pushing each other. They moved words here and there, they argued over what rhymed with what, they thought they would never finish. But as the bell rang again, it was done. They were all smiles as they returned to class.

"Now it is Themba's turn," said Mrs Draper.

Themba moved to the front of the class, hitched up his trousers, blinked and began:

"May I do it like Alan did his, Miss?"

"Of course, Themba."

"I am of leather and once was a hide,
Salted and softened, and not very wide.
Put *me* to your ear and you will hear
Sounds from afar, ringing clear . . ."

"Miss! It's another sort of . . ."

"Shh . . . go on, Themba."

Themba had started off well, but now he was nervous. His notebook started to shake in his hand.

"I'm a funnel, I can trap frogs,
I've even been used to silence the dogs!
I'm a scoop, a cap, and I can hold stones,
I am so much, they offer me thrones!"

Silence.

Heads turned towards each other, then all looked at Mrs Draper to see if she had guessed.

"Read it again, Themba, please," someone asked.

Themba, more at ease now, winked at Alan, and read the verse again.

"Well, children, do you give up?" Mrs Draper looked around the class.

More silence.

"You've got them this time, Themba. And me too. Will you show us what it is, please?"

"In Zululand," said Themba with a slow smile, "long ago when many leather shields were still made, there were always small pieces left over. The old men made many little things from the off-cuts, mostly for the children."

He opened his parcel and produced a sort of leather funnel, neatly stitched, and with the point sliced away.

"The children use them in lots of games, and when you put one to your ear you can hear the sounds of the valleys. It is called *uphondo*. This one belonged to my father. He gave it to me."

Mrs Draper clapped her hands, and the children joined in.

Themba's Bring and Tell was judged best, and Mrs Draper called him up to her desk to receive his star.

"Alan should get one too, Miss," said Themba. Alan dropped his eyes and went red in the face. After a moment he looked up and found Themba staring at him. Their eyes held, and they smiled a secret smile at each other.

"You see, Miss," said Themba, "Alan did most of the poem."

"Really? Come up here then, Alan," said Mrs Draper.

And Alan, standing next to Themba, received a star too. The class clapped and cheered, and everybody crowded around them, wanting to see and touch and hear the shell and especially *uphondo*.

After school Alan and Themba walked away together, talking twenty to the dozen. "Gee! This is nearly as good as Uvongo," said Alan, happily thumping Themba on the back.

"Well," said Themba, "I told you – seek and . . ."

". . . you will find!" Alan was quick to add.

ILSE ANDRAG
Anna's magic stick

ILLUSTRATED BY TERRY MILNE

ANNA SIGHED. School was over but she felt miserable. Just plain miserable. It was as hot as could be, and here she was walking along the road in socks and shoes and a sweaty blazer.

It had been a horrible day at school. The Sub B teacher was much stricter than her Sub A teacher from last year. Everyone in the class had at least one cross against their name on the punishment chart that Mrs Barking had stuck to the wall with some Prestik.

The worst thing about Mrs Barking was that you didn't even know that you were doing anything wrong, and still she gave you a cross. Anna had got her first one the day before. When the intercom began to crackle with announcements, she asked Greta in a whisper for her sharpener. Then, when the announcements were over, Mrs Barking called out: "Anna Grey, you shouldn't be talking while Mr Maree announces something. Go and put a cross against your name!"

Now Anna was nearly home. She lived in a street where the bright green leaves of the oak trees met overhead and rustled against each other. There was a water furrow alongside the pavement. Every day Anna took off her shoes and socks and walked in the cool water. Her house had a long driveway, and halfway up it was the most wonderful climbing tree in the world. It had hundreds of branches so that you could climb almost to heaven. And as you climbed you were enfolded in the soft green of the leaves.

Anna crept in under the lower branches. Usually, if she was lucky, she would come to the tree as soon as she'd changed out of her school clothes and eaten her lunch. But if she was unlucky, she would hear: "Anna, hang up your school clothes!" or "Anna, have you practised your recorder yet?" or even worse: "Where are my nail-scissors, Anna?" or "Why haven't you put your clothes in the washbasket, Anna?"

This afternoon, she simply couldn't face her mother's nagging.

So plop! she dropped her schoolbag onto the ground, and climbed quickly into the tree. Her favourite place was three quarters of the way up. Here no one could get to her.

She sat with her arms round the rough bark and looked out over the houses. She sighed and said aloud: "Why is it so hard being young? I wish I could do magic! I wish I could do magic on myself so that everything I did was right instead of wrong. I wish I could do magic so that there were no more cross words ever again . . ."

"You can," Anna heard from beneath. She looked down through the branches. Someone was sitting on the ground below! It was a little old man with a long grey beard. She climbed down a bit so that she could see him better. When the old man looked up, Anna found she was looking into the friendliest of faces, full of fine wrinkles. She saw his clothes were tattered and grey like the tree trunk, and his sandals were dusty as if he'd walked very far on rough roads.

"You can," the old man repeated. "Look

43

here at this stick. It's a magic stick." Anna climbed down further, and he held out a smooth wooden stick as long and thick as her father's middle finger. "This magic stick will help you," the old man said. "Every time you feel scared or miserable, or when something is threatening you, put your hand in your pocket and hold the stick. Whatever was horrible will become better straight away, but then the power of the stick will have been used up. To charge it again, you will have to do something good. Then the stick will be ready for the next time you need it."

Anna took the stick shyly and put it into her pocket. "Thank you," she said. "I must go and have my lunch. Thank you very much," and she slid from the branch to the ground.

"Goodbye," she said softly to the old man, who sat peacefully leaning against the tree trunk. He smiled and nodded. He really did look just like the grey bark, she thought.

When she crept out from beneath the lower branches, her mother was standing on the stoep with her hands on her hips. Anna's heart skipped a beat, but then she remembered the magic stick. She grabbed hold of it and at once something wonderful happened! The impatient look on her mother's face changed to a friendly one.

"Hello, my angel!" her mother said. "I've just been wondering where you were. I've made you a special chicken sandwich. Was Mrs Larkin a bit nicer in class today?"

Anna put her arms round her mother and hugged her. She wished her mother could always be like this.

But when she got to her room, she saw her bed wasn't made and there were things lying all over the floor. The old dreadful feeling of misery came over her. She sank down onto her bed. Then she remembered the magic stick. But its power was all used up! So she would have to do something good to charge it again. She undressed quickly, hung up her school clothes, put away the things that were lying on the floor and made her bed. Now she felt much better.

The next morning Anna made certain that the magic stick was in her pocket. When Mrs Barking walked into the classroom, Anna gripped the stick even before anything horrid could happen.

The Sub Bs all stood up straight. They were waiting for the first angry word.

Suddenly the Prestik gave way and the chart with the crosses fell plonk! on the floor.

"Ha-ha-ha!" Mrs Barking, of all people, burst out laughing. Then the whole class joined her. They really shrieked with laughter!

Mrs Barking picked up the chart and put it on an empty shelf. "Let's forget about crosses today and see how we get on without them. Today can be Work Together Day. You work along with me and I with you. If it goes well, then we'll try it again tomorrow."

Of course no one knew of the magic stick, but Anna made sure that she did something to recharge it. After their cut-and-glue lesson, she got Greta to collect the scissors, and she went round with the wastepaper basket so that everyone could throw their scraps of paper into it.

That afternoon, when Anna was having lunch with her mother, she asked: "Mum, why do you always call her Mrs Larkin? Isn't it Mrs Barking?"

"No, silly," her mother laughed, "it's Larkin – an old-fashioned word meaning a baby lark."

"Ah!" said Anna. "I always thought it was Mrs Barking. But in any case, from today she doesn't bark any more. She's as happy as a baby lark!"

And only Anna knew why!

D H

JOHANNA MORULE
Mpipidi and the motlopi tree

ILLUSTRATED BY ZWELETHU MTHETHWA

ONCE THERE WAS a boy called Mpipidi. He lived in a small village, far out in the country where the motlopi trees grow and jackals howl at night. Mpipidi lived with his parents and his younger brother. Often he had wished for a sister. But this, his dearest wish, had not come true.

Mpipidi herded his father's cattle. Every morning before the sun rose he would take his provisions and drive the brown herd deep into the bush. Here he climbed into the highest motlopi tree and watched the cattle. He loved sitting up there, where he could see the blue mountains in the distance, and where he was so high up that the eagle was his brother and the cloud was his sister. His sister? The thought made him sad.

When one of the cows strayed, Mpipidi would whistle softly. He whistled a sweet, haunting tune, like that of the honeybird calling a badger to a honeycomb.

Then Mpipidi would chant:

> "Tswerr, tswerr!
> My brown ones
> Do not stray
> Tswerr, tswerr!
> Or you'll be swallowed
> By kgokgomodumo!
> Tswerr, tswerr!"

Then the stray cow would lift its head and would return, grazing, towards Mpipidi in the motlopi tree. This magic saved Mpipidi the trouble of climbing up and down the tree to look for the cattle.

One day, Mpipidi took the cattle even further into the bush, and while he was looking for the tallest motlopi tree he heard faint crying: "Nngee! Nngee!"

Mpipidi stopped and listened. Yes, there it was again: "Nngee! Nngee!"

He crawled under the dense branches of the motlopi tree and there, in a newly woven basket, padded with soft skins of wild animals, he found a baby. Mpipidi carefully picked up the baby. It was a little girl. His heart beat faster . . . No, he cannot take her home! Perhaps they would not believe his story and give her away. So he put the baby back into the basket and looked for another motlopi tree far away where he could hide her.

Then he took milk from his provisions and fed her. Soon the baby was happy and fell asleep. Mpipidi chopped some branches from thorn trees and laid them around her sleeping place as a fence to protect her from wild animals.

That evening he told nobody about the baby. She remained his secret.

Every morning, from that day onwards, Mpipidi would take some goat's milk for the baby and some food for himself. Every morning he would drive the cattle deep into the bush. He would carefully approach the motlopi tree, and when he was near, he would softly sing:

46

"A ga anke a lela –
Tshetsanyane – tshetsa!
Ngwanaa 'tlhare sa motlopi –
Tshetsanyane – tshetsa!
Motlopi le Mpipidi –
Tshetsanyane – tshetsa!
Ako a l'le a ree: Nngee!
Tshetsanyane – tshetsa!"

A little voice answered: "Nngee! Nngee!" and Mpipidi would know that the baby was still alive. He would remove one of the fencing branches, pick her up and feed her, singing all the while. When the baby was well fed, he would carefully put her back into the basket under the motlopi tree and cover her with the skins. Then he would replace the fencing branch.

This continued until his mother guessed that Mpipidi had a secret. So she said to her husband: "What do you think about this boy? Why does he insist on following the cattle every day, even if the weather is bad?"

The father added: "And why doesn't he want his brother to go with him? How will his brother ever learn to look after the cattle? I will follow him tomorrow morning!"

The next morning, the father followed Mpipidi. He stayed far enough behind him not to be seen, but near enough to hear his son's whistling and singing.

Mpipidi drove the cattle into the grazing place, whistling all the way.

Deep in the bush, the whistling stopped. The father walked a little faster and saw how Mpipidi carefully approached the tall motlopi tree. When he was near the tree, the father heard him sing softly:

"A ga anke a lela –
Tshetsanyane – tshetsa!
Ngwanaa 'tlhare sa motlopi –
Tshetsanyane – tshetsa!
Motlopi le Mpipidi –
Tshetsanyane – tshetsa!
Ako a l'le a ree: Nngee!
Tshetsanyane – tshetsa!"

Then the father heard the little voice: "Nngee! Nngee!" His heart beat faster. His eyes widened. Wasn't that a baby's cry?

He saw Mpipidi remove one of the fencing branches, pick up a baby and feed it. When the baby was well fed, Mpipidi carefully put her back into the basket under the tree and covered her with the skins. Then he replaced the fencing branch.

So this was his son's secret! The father immediately returned home and told his wife what he had seen.

The next morning, while it was still dark, Mpipidi's father took his wife to the motlopi tree. Long before anyone else in the village was awake, they were back with the baby.

As usual Mpipidi took his provisions and the goat's milk and drove the cattle deep into the bush. Carefully he approached the tall motlopi tree. When he was near the tree, he softly sang his song. He listened, but there was no little voice. He repeated the tune. Still no answer. His voice trembled as he sang again and again. Only dead silence came from the motlopi tree.

So Mpipidi pulled away the branches – but the baby was gone! He lay down under the motlopi tree and cried bitterly. In the afternoon he drove the cattle back home.

When he got home, he went into the hut and sat down so that the smoke from the open fire stung his eyes. Tears rolled down his cheeks and his heart was heavy with fear and sorrow.

"Why are you crying, Mpipidi?" his mother asked. He told her his eyes were smarting from the smoke. But when she asked him to go out into the fresh air, Mpipidi only shook his head.

"Mpipidi," said his mother, "we know that you are crying for the baby you had hidden under the motlopi tree."

Mpipidi was shocked, and he stopped crying.

"Come with me," his mother said. And she called his father too. She carefully approached the sleeping-hut. At the door, she softly sang:

"A ga anke a lela –
Tshetsanyane – tshetsa!
Ngwanaa 'tlhare sa motlopi –
Tshetsanyane – tshetsa!
Motlopi le Mpipidi –
Tshetsanyane – tshetsa!
Ako a l'le a ree: Nngee!
Tshetsanyane – tshetsa!"

Then they heard the little voice: "Nngee! Nngee!"

Mpipidi looked at his mother. Then he looked at his father. "Yes, Mpipidi," said his father, "we know that was your secret! Was that why you did not want your brother to herd the cattle with you?"

Mpipidi did not answer. He took the bottle and sat down to feed the baby as usual.

His mother gazed at him and saw how much he loved the baby.

"Give me Keneilwe – your baby sister," she said. Mpipidi gave her the baby. He was filled with deep joy to see his sister in his mother's arms.

Keneilwe grew up to be a beautiful girl and a loving sister. Her name reminded everyone of her strange beginnings. Keneilwe – "the one who is given".

Traditional story of the Batswana

MOTLOPI LE MPIPIDI

A ga a-nke a le-la / Tshet-sa-nyane, tshetsa!

Ngwanaa 'tlhare sa mo-tlopi / Tshet-sa-nyane, tshetsa!

Mot-lo-pi le Mpipi-di / Tshet-sa-nyane, tshetsa!

A-ko a l'le a ree: Ngee, Ngee! Tshet-sa-nyane, tshetsa!

Hans Bodenstein.

49

RONA RUPERT
A Children's Calendar

ILLUSTRATED BY ALIDA BOTHMA

January

Dear Lord
I am a fish.
Protect me
    from churning blades of ships
    and hooks and nets
    set to haul me from the sea.
Help me
    to forgive my enemies
and to remember
    that you rule the waters
    and the fish
    that live in them.
AMEN

February

Dear Lord
I am a grapevine,
    an ordinary hanepoot
    that bears green bunches.
Protect me
    from the blade of the axe,
    from blight and disease.
Let me forgive
    those who neglect me.
Help me to remember
    that you created the sweetness of life
    – and me.
AMEN

March

Dear Lord
I am a swallow
    and I follow the summer.
Protect me
    from hawks and hail
    and snares and guns.
Help me to forgive
    those who shatter my nest with stones
and to remember
    that birds are like angels,
    with wings to soar
    through the heavenly sky.
AMEN

50

April

Dear Lord
I am a sheep,
　　my home is the Karoo.
Protect me
　　from the knife of the butcher
　　and the jackal at night.
Help me forgive my tormentors
and let me remember
　　that all creatures are in your hands:
　　those that are clever and strong
　　and those that are weak and dumb
　　like me.
AMEN

May

Dear Lord
I am an oak tree
　　and now my branches are bare.
Protect me
　　from lightning and storms
and wake me up in spring
　　when the arums bloom.
Help me to forgive those
　　who fell trees
and help me remember
　　that You count every brown leaf
　　that falls.
AMEN

June

Dear Lord
I am a castaway cat
　　and I live off lizards and rats.
Protect me from dogs and fleas,
　　from cat-flu and rain
　　and wheels of cars.
Help me to forgive my enemies
and to remember
　　that Your mercy is so great
　　that even a cat
　　can find warmth
　　in its folds.
AMEN

July

Dear Lord
I am a duiker
   harmless and small.
Protect me
   from lions and wildfire
   and the man with a gun
   who shoots for fun.
Let me forgive them
and help me remember
   that because you are faithful to all
   I too will be cared for
   by You.
AMEN

August

Dear Lord
I am a daisy.
Protect me
   from trampling feet
   and scorching winds
   and drought and sleet.
Let fields of flowers
   sprout from my seeds.
Help me to forgive my enemies
and let me remember
   that I too have a place
   on this earth.
AMEN

September

Dear Lord
I am a horse.
Protect me from lashes
   and heavy loads,
   from hunger and thirst
   and a stone in my hoof.
Let me forgive the rider
   and his whip
and let me remember
   that for every uphill in life
   a downhill follows
   as a gift from You.
AMEN

October

Dear Lord
I am a bee
   toiling from daybreak till dusk,
   gathering nectar and pollen.
Protect me
   from ants and bee-eaters
   and laziness and anger.
Help me to forgive those who rob our honey
   to sell it for money
and let me remember
   that even a bee with a sting
   needs to trust in You.
AMEN

November

Dear Lord
I am a baboon
   and live in a zoo.
Protect me
   from boredom and loneliness
   and children that tease me.
Comfort me when I long
   for my mother in the mountain
and let me forgive my captors.
Help me remember
   that even a clown like me
   is safe in Your hand.
AMEN

December

Dear Lord
I am a child
   blessed by You
   with flowers and sunshine and rain,
   a home and people who look after me.
Protect me
   when I am afraid at night.
Help me to forgive
   those who make me angry
and let me never forget
   that You love all things on earth
   including me.
AMEN   HB

GEORGE WEIDEMAN
Bastian, Beauty and Daffodil the goat

ILLUSTRATED BY ANN WALTON

BASTIAN USED TO live on a farm.

There were soft woolly sheep and a horse that rolled in the river sand. There were chickens and stroppy goats that Bastian had to chase out of the garden.

But above all there was the horse. Bastian's horse. Its name was Twilight.

Then came the drought. The Great Drought. The mealies dried up. The grass shrivelled to patches of stubble. The river became a dust path.

Most of the farmers had to sell everything. Bastian's father was one of them.

It was a sad time.

Bastian's father felt heartsore because he had to part with his tractor. His mother cried because she didn't know where she'd get goat's milk for Bastian's baby sister. Other milk made her sick. But for Bastian the hardest was when his father told him one evening that they would have to sell Twilight.

"Twilight is old," his mother tried to comfort him.

"A big boy of nine doesn't cry when an old horse gets sold," his father said – and looked far away over the veld.

Bastian didn't care about being big. He pressed his face into his pillow.

"The man who wants to buy Twilight has plenty of fodder," his mother said. "We don't have any. Look how dry it is."

Even though it was true, Bastian didn't want to hear it.

They moved into a small flat above a garage at the edge of the town. His mother had to hang up her washing on the cement roof. His father worked in the garage.

From the roof, Bastian could just see the mealie-fields of the people who lived on the plots. Sometimes he even saw a horse. The plots were all around the town, just like hundreds of little farms. But not one of these belonged to them.

The only soil they had was in a basin next to the back door of the flat. In it was their only bit of greenery: a geranium that didn't seem to feel like flowering yet.

Then, one Saturday, Bastian's mother sent him to the Post Office. It was a long way, but he didn't have money for the bus fare. Since the Great Drought there had been very little money for anything.

So he had to walk.

Bastian saw the goat on his way back from the post office. Suddenly, there she was, between the circling cars and the whizzing bicycles . . . standing on a traffic island in the middle of the main road.

He rubbed his eyes. Could it really be true? But when he took his hands away, there she was still. Standing quite happily with a frayed piece of rope around her neck. She must have broken loose from somewhere.

What on earth was a goat doing on a traffic island?

As if she had read his thoughts, the goat looked up at him over a mouthful of grass. Her jaws went from side to side as she chewed.

A double-decker bus and three lorries stopped at the traffic light. They hid her from

54

view. But when they pulled away she was still there.

Someone is going to knock her down, thought Bastian, and he waited his turn. When the traffic light turned green he dashed across the street. He hoped she wouldn't start running!

"What are you doing here?" he asked. The goat stood as if she hadn't a care in the world. Her yellow eyes seemed to say: "And what does it matter to you?"

Bastian crouched down. And now? he thought. I've crossed the road. I can't just go back. Whose goat can it be?

"Hey! Do you think this is some sort of farm?" a lorry driver called out.

What could he do with the goat?

"Does she give good milk, farm-boy?" someone else shouted.

That's it! My baby sister! They're having trouble getting goat's milk. And it's expensive.

Bastian put his hand out towards the goat.

"Please don't run away," he murmured softly as he stroked her back. She shivered with pleasure.

"You can't stay here," he said. "Someone will catch you and slaughter you. Or the lorries will make mincemeat of you." The goat snorted as if in agreement. Bastian made a decision.

He would take her. But where to?

She couldn't stay on top of the garage. A goat needed grass. His mother couldn't drag her up and down the steps every day. The goat would eat the geranium plant and tear the washing off the line on the roof.

But she couldn't stay here either.

They reached the pavement safely. The flat was a long way away and the goat made him tired. She was "otherwise". That's what Bastian's mother always said about him, when he didn't want to do things.

"Come on, you otherwise goat!" he said, when the goat stopped to nibble at a piece of paper. "It looks as if you eat anything!"

Outside a café the people laughed at him.

"Do you perhaps know whom the goat belongs to?" he asked the owner of the café, a fat man with a moustache.

"No!" snapped the man. "Take the creature away. He smells!"

"It's a she, not a he," Bastian said. And as if the goat was also offended, she nibbled a serviette off one of the tables.

"Scram! Or I'll call the police!" The man rushed at them. But he pulled up short as the goat dropped her head and threatened him with her horns.

"Behave yourself, or there'll be trouble," Bastian whispered to her and dragged her away.

In front of a butcher's shop stood a blockman with a dark blue-and-white striped apron.

"Hey!" he called as he sharpened his butcher's knife on the cement step. "Where did you get such a nice fat goat?" He disappeared through the doorway as if he thought Bastian and the goat would follow. Bastian pulled as hard as he could at the goat, which had discovered a patch of grass. "Come on,

stupid thing! Can't you see that man has his knife out for you?"

At an intersection, the goat pulled hard in the wrong direction. "What are you up to now?" Bastian panted. Then, before he knew what was happening, she was running straight for some fruit and flower stalls.

"You greedy-guts goat! Come here!" he shouted. But it didn't help.

A girl of about his own age helped Bastian steer the goat away from the flowers and fruit, but not before the goat had managed to devour a bunch of flowers.

"Look at that! You demon! There goes my best bunch of daffodils! And my profit!" a woman shouted.

The girl tied the goat to a pole. "What's your name?" she asked Bastian when she was sure the goat was secure.

"Bastian," he answered a little shakily. "And yours?"

"Beauty."

"That's a strange name."

"Bastian sounds just as strange to me." She wrinkled her nose. "And the goat?"

"She doesn't have a name."

"My mother is very cross with your goat," Beauty said. "She's eaten her best daffodils."

Bastian told Beauty how he had found the goat. He also told her about the farm and about Twilight.

"Let's give the goat a name," Beauty said. "I know! Daffodil! Because she ate my mother's flowers."

"Two bunches for six rand," her mother called out. "Lovely daffodils!" She found some broken leaves and stems between the buckets and held them out to the goat. Bastian saw that she was smiling. She didn't look nearly as cross any more.

He leant against the pole and rubbed Daffodil's head. He told Beauty about his baby sister and the goat's milk. "And then I found the goat," he said. "But we live in a flat . . ."

"We don't have a goat," Beauty said. "But we do have grass."

"Do you mean . . ." Bastian started to say. "Where do you stay?" he asked eagerly.

"We live on a farm on the other side of town," Beauty replied. "It's not really a farm. Just a plot."

"I can see the plots from our flat," Bastian said.

"I've got a plan," Beauty said. "Daffodil can come and stay with us. My father can help us fence off a place for her. And then you'll always have milk for your little sister."

"How far away do you live?"

Beauty told him. It didn't seem to be very far from the flat. But it was certainly too far to walk.

"There's a broken bicycle at the garage where my father works," Bastian said. "Perhaps he'll be able to fix it and I'll ride across to you."

"Then I can learn to ride a bicycle too!" said Beauty.

And that's how Daffodil found herself two keepers who cared for her – Bastian and Beauty – and she was never "otherwise" again.   D H

IAIN MACDONALD
Dreaming of dragons

ILLUSTRATED BY JOAN RANKIN

KEVIN'S MOTHER had always told him there were no dragons. So had his teacher. Dragons are only in stories, they said.

But here he was – face to face with a real, scary, fire-snorting dragon! He was standing with his back to the sea, with the dragon roaring down the beach towards him, and he held what looked like a magic sword in his hand. Jewels flashed on its hilt and there was strange writing on the blade. It read: 𝕴 𝖆𝖒 𝕯𝖗𝖆𝖌𝖔𝖓𝖘𝖑𝖆𝖞𝖊𝖗. 𝕭𝖚𝖙 𝖜𝖍𝖎𝖘𝖙𝖑𝖊 𝖇𝖊𝖋𝖔𝖗𝖊 𝖞𝖔𝖚 𝖚𝖘𝖊 𝖒𝖊.

Kevin felt something cold in his other hand – it was a small silver flute! And as he glanced at the flute, he remembered in a flash how he had got there . . .

There had been a big wind from the north-west, bringing in cold winter weather, and he'd been sitting by the fireplace, watching as his dad put some firewood on the fire. The warmth and crackle of the fire made him sleepy, so he'd stretched out and gone into the garden for some fresh air.

Even though it was cold outside it was a beautiful night, and the stars were clear as polished silver in the velvet sky. He was walking on the grass, looking up to see if he could find the Southern Cross, when suddenly, without warning, he found himself falling.

Down and down he went, almost floating through what seemed to be a deep, deep hole in the ground. He didn't feel scared at all. Then, with a splash, he found himself in a warm blue sea, swimming towards the nearby beach. The beach seemed a little brighter than most beaches, the sand shimmering like gold dust.

He swam ashore, and there, stuck into the shimmering sand, he'd seen the jewelled sword, with a little flute hanging from its handle on a silver chain . . .

And now this terrible dragon was coming roaring at him . . . big and green and scaly, with a huge, lumpy head and big claws and a lashing tail. But glancing at the flute, Kevin saw written on it: 𝕭𝖑𝖔𝖜 𝖒𝖊 𝖎𝖋 𝖞𝖔𝖚 𝖓𝖊𝖊𝖉 𝖍𝖊𝖑𝖕.

So he lifted the magic flute to his lips and blew hard.

And as he did so, he heard the answering

58

whistle of another flute behind him. He swung round – and there was a small boat with a single sail coming fast to shore. In the boat was a strange little man who waved cheerfully to Kevin.

"Come on! Get in quickly!" he shouted, bringing the boat close to the beach.

Kevin splashed through the waves, still clutching the sword and the flute. "Phew, thanks!" he said, much relieved. Then, looking back at the dragon as it roared down to the water's edge, whipping up clouds of golden sand and blowing furious black smoke from its nostrils, he asked: "Won't the dragon follow us?"

The little man shook his head.

"Oh no," he said. "Dragons are like cats. They don't like to get their feet wet." Then he turned the sail deftly and the boat shot out to sea, leaving the dragon roaring and belching smoke on the beach.

Kevin looked at the quaint little man. He had a small white beard, a sailor's cap, and on his neat leather waistcoat tiny bells jingled merrily in the breeze. He wore blue sailor's trousers and had soft leather boots on his feet.

"Who are you, and where am I, and where are we going?" Kevin asked.

"My name is Electron, you're in the Dragon Islands and we're going to the helicopter to take you home," the little bearded man said with a smile.

"But how did I get here?" Kevin asked.

"You fell down a time-hole. Quite a few people do. That's why we leave swords and flutes in some places on the beach in case people find themselves in trouble with a dragon. Dragons can be real pests, you know."

"And what do you do here?" Kevin asked.

"I'm one of the Ember Elves, and my job is rescuing visitors like yourself, mostly. And if you want to know about the Ember Elves, well, we're here because of the volcano. I suppose you want to know all about that too?" he asked, glancing at Kevin with a merry twinkle in his eyes.

"Oh yes. I like volcanoes," Kevin said. "They can spit fire."

"Well, you shouldn't. When volcanoes get too hot, they shake the world above, from where you come. So we have to plant things to keep the soil up there from shaking apart. And to make things pretty. We're planting orchids now, mostly," he said.

"Why do you have to plant things? Don't they just grow by themselves?" Kevin asked.

Electron sighed and stroked his white beard. "I suppose your teacher or your parents have been telling you that. But we elves are really the ones who make things grow. We scatter seeds by night from our helicopter and water them with dew or sea mist."

"That's not what I heard," said Kevin.

"I'll bet your teacher and your mom and dad told you there weren't really dragons either, eh?" Electron said.

"That's true," Kevin said thoughtfully.

He was about to ask more questions, but they were getting close to another island, and he saw a big helicopter on the launching pad near the shore. A group of elves, looking just like Electron, were busily scurrying about, loading boxes and sacks into it.

As they pulled the boat in to shore, Kevin saw that the strange writing on the boxes was the same as that on the sword and the flute. The writing said: Orchids. Wild Flowers. Cape Fynbos. Assorted Seeds.

But he did not have much time to look around, because the helicopter's engine had started with a roar and the other elves were calling them over to it. Electron and Kevin climbed inside and the helicopter took off with a whoosh.

The elf pilot aimed its nose upwards at what seemed to be a hole in the sky, a blue patch with jagged cloud edges that got bigger and bigger as they came closer. When Kevin looked down, he could see a volcano on one of the green islands far, far below, spitting out smoke and red sparks.

Then the helicopter shot through the hole in the sky and they were suddenly in darkness. Looking out of the window Kevin saw the familiar shape of the Southern Cross among the stars. Then, after whizzing along for some time, the helicopter began to descend. It hovered for a while, then landed right in Kevin's garden.

Electron opened the door and Kevin climbed out. "You'd better give me those," Electron said, pointing to the magic flute and the jewelled sword in Kevin's hands. Otherwise your mum and dad will start asking questions."

Kevin did so, and Electron pushed a small paper packet into his hand. On it, written in that strange old writing, were the words: 𝕰𝖚𝖑𝖔𝖕𝖍𝖎𝖆 𝕻𝖊𝖙𝖊𝖗𝖘𝖎𝖎. 𝕺𝖗𝖈𝖍𝖎𝖉 𝕾𝖊𝖊𝖉𝖘.

"These are for you. Tell me how they're doing when we meet again," Electron said with a smile. Then he waved, closed the door and the helicopter took off.

Kevin waved goodbye. It seemed as if the helicopter was fading into light, a light that got brighter and brighter so that he had to shield his eyes . . .

The bedroom door opened and his mother came in with a glass of orange juice.

"Morning, sleepy head," she said.

"How did I get here?" Kevin asked.

His mother ruffled his hair.

"You fell asleep in front of the fire and your father carried you to bed. Don't you remember?"

She put the orange juice down next to the bed, and as she did so, she said: "What's this?"

On Kevin's bedside table was a small packet. And written on it in strange old writing were the words: 𝕰𝖚𝖑𝖔𝖕𝖍𝖎𝖆 𝕻𝖊𝖙𝖊𝖗𝖘𝖎𝖎. 𝕺𝖗𝖈𝖍𝖎𝖉 𝕾𝖊𝖊𝖉𝖘.

Kevin was surprised, but he picked up the packet and looked at it. So it hadn't just been a dream after all . . .

"It's some seeds I want to plant for a friend," he said.

Then he smiled at his mother.

"Are you *sure* you don't believe in dragons?" he asked.

DIANNE HOFMEYR
Thelma, the Three Rackets and the Magic Moment Club

ILLUSTRATED BY BRANDAN REYNOLDS

THELMA MAKWELA KWELA loved to dance and sing. Every evening she put on a glittery dress, made a special hairstyle, and then she danced and sang the night away at the Magic Moment Club. And every evening people came from all over to hear her sing and watch her dance. Then, when the roosters started to crow, Thelma went home and tumbled into bed and slept right through the rest of the day.

All that would have been fine if Thelma hadn't got two new neighbours. She had hardly tumbled into bed one morning when she heard a great thumping noise coming from the wall next to her bed. She peeped through a chink in the wall . . . Oh no! A drummer had moved in next door to her.

Ta . . . tarat ta ta . . . tum!

Ta . . . tarat ta ta . . . tum!

She covered her head with a pillow to block out the taratantara of his drumming. But she got very little sleep, and that night she found it hard to sing and dance as well as usual at the Magic Moment Club. Her feet were slow and her voice was sleepy.

The next morning – just when she tumbled into bed – the taratantara started up again. So she banged on the wall.

"Stop the racket!" she shouted. "I'm trying to sleep!"

But it didn't help. The drummer just tara-tantara-ed his drums even louder . . . all day long.

Ta . . . tarat ta ta . . . tum!

Ta . . . tarat ta ta . . . tum!

This went on for weeks and weeks, Thelma

singing and dancing all night long and the drummer thumping all day long. Poor Thelma was exhausted.

One day, even with cotton wool stuffed into her ears and three pillows over her head, she still heard the terrible row. But this time it was worse – there was a charivari coming from below her as well as a taratantara from next door!

When she leant out of her window she saw that a man who played the electric guitar had moved into the flat just below hers.

Cha . . . chi chi, chi chi cha . . . chi chi . . .

Chi, chi, chi, ching . . . ching . . . ching!

"Stop the racket!" she shouted. "I'm trying to sleep!"

But it didn't help. The man just chari-vari-ed his guitar even louder.

Cha . . . chi chi, chi chi cha . . . chi chi . . .

Chi, chi, chi, ching . . . ching . . . ching! – until Thelma thought her head would split. When would she ever be able to sleep?

That night at the Magic Moment Club she

started yawning in the middle of her songs and dragging her feet. And the people who had come from all over to hear her sing and watch her dance made paper aeroplanes of their serviettes and threw them at her.

"This won't do," said the manager. "You're out of a job. You're fired!"

Fired! Oh no! What was she going to do?

"Just give me one more chance," she begged.

"Well . . ." said the manager, thinking about the people who would come from all over to the Magic Moment Club, expecting someone to sing and dance for them. "Well . . . unless you sing better tomorrow night, you're fired!"

Thelma went home very early that morning. Long, long before the roosters started to crow. Instead of tumbling into bed and trying to sleep, she turned her music up as loud as she could and tried her very best to sing and dance like before. But her voice sounded like a rooster with a sore throat. And when she danced, her feet felt like a hundred heavy bricks. The more she tried, the worse it became. She was just too tired.

In the middle of it all, there was a thump on her wall and the drummer called out: "What are you doing?"

"Singing! I'm only singing!"

"Well, stop the racket, I'm trying to sleep!"

Then there was a thud on the floor and the guitar-player called out from below: "What are you doing?"

"Dancing! I'm only dancing!"

"Well, stop the racket, I'm trying to sleep!"

Thelma stamped her feet and danced harder. "I've also been trying to sleep for many mornings now," she yelled.

"Not this morning!" the drummer shouted back. "You've been trying to sing!"

"And you're trying to dance!" shouted the guitar-player. "All over my ceiling!"

"Why can't you dance and sing during the day?" yelled the drummer.

"Yes! Why can't you sleep at night?" yelled the guitar-player.

Suddenly Thelma had a wonderful idea. She rushed next door to the drummer and she told him her idea. Then she rushed downstairs to the guitar-player and she told him as well. Then she tumbled into bed and slept right into the afternoon, because everything was quiet – no drumming, no charivari-ing.

That evening Thelma made an extra-special hairstyle and put extra extra glitter and spangles on her dress. Then off she went in a dazzle to the Magic Moment Club.

And the drummer, Toki, made his best hairstyle and put on his best drumming clothes and off he went to the Magic Moment Club.

And the guitar-player, Tjangi, didn't do anything to his hairstyle because he had shaved off all his hair, but he put on his best guitar-playing clothes and off he went to the Magic Moment Club as well.

There Thelma sang and danced. Toki tara-tantara'ed his drums. And Tjangi charivari-ed his guitar. Together they made the best music that the people who had come from all over to the Magic Moment Club had ever heard. Instead of making paper aeroplanes, they grabbed flowers from the vases on the tables and showered them on Thelma and Tjangi and Toki. And they clapped and cheered and stamped. "You're the best!" they shouted.

The manager begged all three of them, Thelma, Toki and Tjangi, to perform every night from then on.

"But what shall we call your group?" he asked.

"The Three Rackets," Thelma decided.

"The Three Rackets?" the manager questioned.

"Yes, the Three Rackets," Toki and Tjangi agreed.

So the Three Rackets played and danced and sang the rest of the night away.

When the roosters started to crow, Thelma and Toki and Tjangi went home. All three of the Three Rackets tumbled into their beds and fell asleep.

And from then on all three neighbours slept undisturbed right through the quiet days until it was time to get ready for their performance at the Magic Moment Club.

64

LAWRENCE MANZEZULU
The great hunter

ILLUSTRATED BY VUSI MALINDI

SIGODONGO SAT WITH his son Dyudyu under the umnga-tree. Sigodongo was worried, something was killing their sheep. In his youth he had been a great hunter. Songs of praise were still sung for him. But now he was old.

His son Dyudyu was not like his father at all. He was fat and lazy.

"We must go and find this beast," said Sigodongo to his son. Dyudyu said nothing, but he was afraid.

The next day Sigodongo and Dyudyu went to the large rocks in the forest to find the beast that was eating up their wealth. Though he was an old man, Sigodongo's footsteps were firm, but Dyudyu lagged behind all the way.

Suddenly a leopard pounced on the old man. Sigodongo was clever enough to catch it by the tail. He wrestled it to the ground, clamping his sinewy arms and legs around the leopard's neck and belly.

"Bamba! Bamba! Mfana wam!" Sigodongo shouted.

But Dyudyu was too afraid to help his father hold the leopard. He ran away as fast as he could, shouting: "Ndilambile ndiyagoduka ngoku! I'm hungry! I'm going home now to eat!"

When he got home, he was so hungry from running all the way that he ate a whole calabash of curdled milk, without even thinking of his poor father.

Much later Dyudyu returned to the forest to see what had happened.

His father was still holding on tightly to the leopard. "Khawubam'okumzuzwana, mfana wam! Come hold the leopard down for a little while!" Sigodonga cried when he saw his son.

And Dyudyu thought: I don't need to be afraid any longer. My father is old – if *he* is able to hold the leopard, so can I. The beast must be tired and weak by now.

So Dyudyu took heart and grabbed hold of the leopard.

Then Sigodongo stood back and laughed at his son. "Remember," he said, "if you let it go, it will eat you. Now I am going home for my dinner – and I too will take my time!"

65

ENGELA VAN ROOYEN
The tree

ILLUSTRATED BY TERRY MILNE

ONE DAY A MAN planted a tree high up on a mountain where no one ever came. Each morning he climbed the steep path up the mountain. He carried water to the tree. He watched it grow and he felt very tender towards it.

"Why have you planted that tree so high up?" people wanted to know as they passed along the road below.

"So that no one will reach it," the man replied. "That tree is mine. It's like a child to me. I look after it, and I love it. One day it will look after me. When I'm old I'll sit in its shade and gaze far out over the veld."

Then a stranger with cold eyes came to the man.

"I will stay here," the stranger said.

"Yes, surely," answered the man, because he was a kind man.

The stranger stayed for a long time. He ate the man's hard-earned food and he used all the man's wood for his fires. He made a huge fire every day.

The veld became bare of wood.

The foot of the mountain became bare.

But the man was frightened to say anything, because the stranger ruled in his house.

One day the stranger said: "It's cold. Bring more firewood."

"There's no more wood, you know that," the man replied. "All the trees around have been chopped down."

"Go and chop down your tree at the top of the mountain," said the stranger. "It will give us plenty of wood."

"I can't chop down that tree," said the man. "I planted and tended it. I love that tree. One day I'm going to sit in its shade."

"One day you'll be dead," said the stranger. "Now do as I say, or . . . Enough, here is the axe! Go, chop it down!"

Anger welled up in the man, but when he looked into the stranger's eyes, he was more frightened than ever. He took the axe and climbed the mountain. He began to chop down the tree. His heart felt as if it would break.

The blows of the axe made a rock roll down.

The rock caused a spark.

The spark started a fire in the grass.

The flames rushed towards the tree. They trapped the man. The man was burnt to death together with his tree.

The fire burnt right through the night, until the whole mountain was black and bare.

When the stranger realised that the man would not return, he took the house for himself.

In the spring the rain came. New grass began to sprout on the bare, black mountain.

The grass grew high.

The wind blew through it.

The grass rustled in the wind.

It whispered: "Never listen to the voice of the stranger that says you must kill what you love . . . love . . . love . . ."

DH

GLADYS THOMAS
Searching for Welcome

ILLUSTRATED BY ZWELETHU MTHETHWA

NOPINK AWOKE EARLY that cold June morning. It still seemed unusually dark and quiet. She sat up and rubbed the sleep from her eyes. She looked around at the many mothers and children who lay sleeping on the wooden floor of the big hall. Then slowly she remembered everything . . . The people running blindly through the smoke, the sickening smell of burning blankets and the desperate shouting, the crying of a lost child, the rumbling, shooting Casspirs.

Now everyone felt safe in the church hall, away from the fighting and burning in Crossroads. Nopink rolled up her blanket and placed it neatly against the wall with their other belongings. Then she crawled over to where the grown-ups slept. Her mother stirred when she felt Nopink moving.

"Why are you awake so early, Nopink?" she asked.

"Mother, we must go and look for Welcome. What will become of her?" Nopink whispered.

"Yes, the poor goat. But I cannot go with you, my child. We mothers have to cook soup for the many hungry people here today. Why don't you ask your friend Mandla to help you look for Welcome? But please be very, very careful out there. If they start fighting again, you must hide in the bushes. If they shoot with birdshot, lie flat on the ground and don't move until the police have left," warned her mother, pulling her dress over her head. "If there's trouble, come back immediately."

Nopink stepped softly between the sleeping people in the hall, looking for her friend Mandla. She found him at the other end of the hall. Soon the two of them were walking through the cold morning, the air still heavy with the smell of teargas and the stench of smouldering shacks.

"Where did you get the goat from?" Mandla asked as they walked along the rough gravel road, rubbing their hands to warm them.

"My father was working at the abattoir in Maitland," Nopink answered. "One cold winter night he came home with a little goat under his jacket. We all went wild with excitement and my mother prepared a bottle of milk for the hungry kid. We called her Welcome, and later my mother taught me how to feed her. I loved looking after her. She used to suck at my fingers sometimes. Welcome grew up into a big nanny-goat. You should see her big titties, which I used to milk every day. Now she's gone and I miss her so much!"

"Don't worry, we'll find her. Someone must have cut her rope when our homes were burnt down. I'm sure she ran away and is hiding somewhere," said Mandla to comfort her.

Soon they reached the sand dunes and burnt-out shacks. They called Welcome's name as loudly as they could, but only a lone, lost dog howled in the distance. As they walked on they passed a few people, some carrying bundles of blankets and furniture on their heads, others collecting blackened corrugated iron sheets and half-burnt poles to rebuild their homes.

Then they reached the site where Nopink's

home had stood. Smoke was still rising from the pile of roofing iron, and under a twisted metal door they could see her mother's burnt-out bedstead. Nopink suddenly felt completely deserted. She turned away quickly, and they walked on until they reached Lansdowne Road. Mandla stopped suddenly, and then Nopink heard it too – an angry rumble that crept nearer and nearer.

Terrified, they crouched down behind a clump of Port Jackson willows. A convoy of army trucks and Casspirs packed with soldiers and police thundered past. Like people going to a war, Nopink thought. The sand was wet under her and she felt Mandla's body trembling next to hers.

After the convoy had passed, they darted across the road.

Deeper in the bush, in a clearing, they found some families who were hiding from the terrible things that were happening in Crossroads. They saw mothers breast-feeding their babies, with nothing but a few bundles of clothing at their feet.

"Have you seen my goat?" Nopink asked the people time and again. But no one had seen Welcome.

Then they came upon a dam of muddy water with oil drums and plastic bags floating on it. But there was no sign of Welcome. Mandla went searching for tadpoles, while Nopink walked around the edge of the dam, poking listlessly at the plastic bags with a long stick.

Mischievously, Mandla crept up behind and pushed Nopink forward into the water. She screamed, struggling to keep her balance, and Mandla pulled her back quickly. She was furious with him, and sat down on the grass and sulked. They were tired and both sat in silence for a while.

Suddenly they heard the stuttering of a goat. "Blaa! Blaaa!"

They jumped up and ran towards the sound, and there, behind an old drum among the trees, stood Welcome, her black-and-white coat dirty and splattered with mud.

The goat looked at Nopink with her big yellow eyes. "Blaa!" she called again.

Nopink threw her arms around the animal's neck and kissed her on her black lips. She was beside herself with happiness. Mandla found an old tin and brought Welcome some water. It seemed that she had had sufficient grass to eat, as her udder hung heavy with milk.

Nopink and Mandla took Welcome back over Lansdowne Road to Crossroads, walking her cautiously so as not to cause her discomfort. The goat followed them meekly, keeping to Nopink's heels. Over the sand dunes they struggled with her, until they eventually arrived at the church hall.

All the children and their mothers came out to see the goat. Nopink milked her while the other children looked on curiously. She was both proud and happy, and she handed the first jug of goat's milk to a mother whose baby was sick. The women said that the fresh goat's milk would surely make the baby well again.

That night Nopink let Welcome sleep next to her in a corner of the church hall. The day had ended well after all. Welcome was back, and soon the baby would be better again. "Dear God, let peace and quiet return to Crossroads, so that Father can begin to build us a new home . . ."

GCINA MHLOPHE
The singing dog

ILLUSTRATED BY CORA COETZEE

Sukela ngantsomi
Chosi

A LONG TIME AGO some of the animals who are now enemies were firm friends who lived and hunted together.

Lion had been king of all the animals from the very beginning. They all feared King Lion and obeyed his word. Yet some said that the rabbit could easily have become king if he had not been so small, because Rabbit too was feared.

Oh, he was a clever, cunning little creature! Many animals had been tricked by Rabbit or hurt by him in one way or another, and they all hated him. But Rabbit did not worry about all the bad talk that went around. He was quite satisfied with his only friend in the world, the one animal he never teased or hurt: Dog. Dog with the trusting eyes.

Though Rabbit and his friend Dog had lots of fun and played many tricks together, they were very different from each other. Dog always tried not to hurt anybody. But his friend Rabbit, oh, he would not stop at anything!

Many days Dog sat with his friend and reasoned with him. "Rabbit," Dog would say, "you know, you can have plenty of fun without hurting anybody." But Rabbit only listened with one long ear and continued with his mischievous ways. In his heart he knew that the only thing that really gave him pleasure was to tease and humiliate bigger animals. Only Dog was safe from Rabbit's tricks.

Rabbit was particularly fond of his friend because of his specially beautiful singing voice.

When the animals got together in meetings called by King Lion, Dog would stand on a rock and sing out for everyone to hear. Even the birds came down to perch on some low branches to listen to the singing dog. His voice would ring out across the valleys and plains, and proud Rabbit would tell anyone who would listen that Dog was his friend.

Well, one fine spring day Rabbit went away on his own and stayed away all day. Dog did not know where his friend had disappeared to, and he missed him very much. When it got to be late afternoon, Dog really started worrying. He wondered if Rabbit had perhaps been caught and eaten by one of the big animals that hated him.

At last Rabbit came home – not walking, but skipping! Relieved, Dog sat down, wondering what story he was about to hear. He could see from Rabbit's face that he had had a most enjoyable day. "Where have you been all day?" he asked his friend.

Rabbit simply stood there in front of him with a big grin on his face – it stretched from ear to ear.

"Come along with me," he said to Dog. "I'll show you the cleanest and cleverest and most beautiful piggy in the world."

Soon they were on their way, Rabbit skipping ahead, his ears up in the air with excitement and his tail gently bobbing. Dog was close behind his friend, his tail up in the air and his long red tongue lolling as he trotted along. Rabbit was in a great hurry – first they walked fast and then they ran.

Finally they arrived at Pig's house. She was

71

sitting quietly under an umnga tree, waiting. When Dog saw her, he had to agree with his friend, this surely was the prettiest pig ever born! When Piggy saw them she stood up and gave them a big smile. She thought Rabbit looked very handsome with his clear bright eyes and his fur all shiny from being brushed by the wind.

After Hagwana the pig had been introduced to Dog, she offered them something to drink under the umnga tree. Soon Rabbit and Pig sat holding hands and looking into each other's eyes, forgetting all about Dog and the rest of the world. They chatted happily and did not even notice Dog quietly moving away from them. He went to sit on a rock nearby. His trusting eyes rested a little sadly on his best friend, whom he had never seen so happy before.

Dog wanted to do something that would make Rabbit even happier. So he sang a special song for him and Pig:

"Ondibuzayo ndithanda bani
    Ndakumxelela ndithanda yena
    UHagwana wam.

Whoever will ask me whom I love,
I'll tell him I love her,
My only one – Hagwana."

Rabbit was very pleased with his friend and Hagwana the pig could not believe her clean little ears. What a sweet voice Dog had!

Back home that evening at supper, Rabbit could hardly taste his food, he was so lost in a dream. And all they talked about was Pig, Pig, Pig. Dog noticed too that his friend had forgotten all about playing tricks and humiliating other animals.

But then, after visiting Pig a few times and singing for her and Rabbit, Dog got tired of talking about her all the time. He really missed the adventures he had shared with Rabbit before he had met the prettiest pig in the world. And so he told his friend that he would not be going with him again to visit Hagwana.

Rabbit did not complain. He went to visit his loved one alone. But the first question she asked was: "Where is Dog?"

"What do you mean, where is Dog? I am here and I love you." Rabbit tickled her pink piggy-nose and tried not to show he was a little angry.

"Yes, I love you too and I'm happy to see you, but I do miss Dog's beautiful singing."

They sat down and talked and held hands. They laughed and tried to be happy with each other, but something was just not right. They did not enjoy themselves as much as they'd done when Dog was there.

Rabbit went home much earlier than he had planned. He did not like what was happening. And when he got home he convinced Dog that he had to come along the next time. He told Dog that the road was twice as long when he was alone. "I'll go with you," Dog said, "but then you must promise not to talk about Hagwana on the way there or back."

Rabbit agreed, and so the very next day the two friends were on their way again. The little pig was very happy to see them and she asked Dog please to sing for them. So the two lovers sat holding hands and Dog sang:

"Ondibuzayo ndithanda bani
Ndakumxelela ndithanda yena
UHagwana wam."

Pig was most pleased. She held hands with Rabbit – but she only had eyes for Dog! Rabbit saw the look on her face. It seemed to say: "What an amazing creature this Dog is!"

Rabbit was very angry and he felt cheated. For the first time in his life he hated his friend, he wanted to kick him hard between those trusting eyes. But he only smiled and thanked Dog for his song.

When the two friends got home they had a big supper at Rabbit's house. It was a beautiful summer evening. The moon was full and it washed the whole countryside with its cool, magical light. The stars twinkled happily at the two friends as they sat there with their stomachs all filled up.

Then Rabbit suddenly sprang to his feet and told his friend he had a surprise for him. "Just a little something to thank you for everything you have done for me and Ha-gwana," Rabbit said, avoiding Dog's eyes.

"But you are my friend, there's no need to thank me."

"Don't say any more, I have some magic medicine right here. Everyone talks about your voice but this medicine will make it even sweeter. Wait a moment, I'll go and fetch it."

Rabbit disappeared behind a bush and came back pretending to hide something be-hind his back. He asked Dog to sit still beside their favourite rock under the umnga tree, to close his eyes and to open his mouth wide so that Rabbit could pour the medicine down his throat.

The trusting friend did as he was told. Rab-bit hopped on top of the rock, and then he pulled out four long white thorns of the umnga tree. He bent down and scratched Dog's throat so hard with the thorns that Dog felt the most terrible pain.

"Awoooo! Awoooo! What have you done to my voice?" Dog cried out hoarsely. "Now it's rough! You've made my voice rough rrough, rrrough!"

He jumped up, barking from pain and anger. He chased after Rabbit, but soon there was no sign of that cunning animal. What Rabbit had seen in Dog's eyes was worse than anything he had ever seen before! He knew right away that Dog would kill him if he didn't get away first.

That beautiful night with a full moon saw the end of their friendship. And Dog never re-covered his sweet singing voice. All he is left with is a rough, harsh bark, and he now chases every rabbit that crosses his path.

Phela – phela ngantsomi.

GEORGE WEIDEMAN
Thandiwe of Khayalethu Camp

ILLUSTRATED BY BRANDAN REYNOLDS

THANDIWE RAN AS fast as she could.

If she could only get to her grandmother and grandfather before the thing caught up with her! She glanced back. The bakkie nose-dived into a shallow ditch. The wheels spun in the sand as it came out again – big wheels that could flatten anything.

Her grandfather was blind and her grand-mother could hardly walk, her back was so bent and sore with years of hard work. They lived on the far edge of the squatter camp, near the big trees and the open veld.

Thandiwe knew that other bakkies were driving through Khayalethu Camp as well. She'd seen them arrive early that morning after her mother and father had gone to work. She was alone – Sipho and Themba had already left before sunrise to look for fire-wood.

First people had screamed. Then she heard the sound of running feet. She heard metal sheets clattering and falling and people shouting to one another. She heard a strange rumbling and when she looked out of the door of their shack, she saw the bakkies coming. Coming with dust that turned the sun dark. Men with guns and crowbars and sledge-hammers.

Thandiwe's heart pounded. She was exhausted. But she dared not stop. She had to warn her blind grandfather and her grand-mother who could no longer walk properly. She had to tell them that the Smashers had arrived.

No one knew who the Smashers were or who sent them and why they were doing it. Or when they would come.

She wondered where everyone had fled to. She thought about the house that her father had put together with so much hard work. Shouldn't she turn back? But then what about her grandfather and grandmother?

A branch scratched her leg and blood ran down it. But she hardly noticed. Her breath came in gasps. It wasn't much further now.

She looked back. The bakkie had come to a standstill. Four big men jumped out. Than-diwe stopped for a moment to catch her breath. She watched as the men attacked a house with crowbars and sledgehammers. She heard the screech of iron ripping apart. She heard wood snapping. She saw the boxes fold. Here and there, coils of black smoke billowed into the air. Her chest felt tight. What if their house was burning too? Perhaps someone had already warned her grandparents. Where would she run to then? Why was it so quiet here?

Themba's teacher in the big school had told them before the school holidays that there was going to be trouble. He told them about the Smashers. But no one in Khayalethu Camp had really believed him.

Themba's teacher had said that the Smashers were people who didn't want them to stay there.

Tsk! thought Thandiwe, we should never have come here! But then she remembered the hunger, the drought and the troubles. In the place where they'd lived only the government people were rich. Very rich. And the poor stayed poor. The drought had eaten all their cattle. That's why they had moved. Now

75

it looked as if they couldn't live here either.

But she dared not think now. She must keep running!

Thandiwe saw her grandparents' shack. The door was closed. Behind her, she knew, the air was full of dust and smoke coming from the smashed and burning houses.

She hammered against the wood-and-iron door.

"It's me, Thandiwe!" she shouted. "Are you there, Grandfather and Grandmother?"

After a moment her grandmother opened the door shakily. "Thandiwe! What's happening? What's all this noise?"

She told her grandparents. Her grandmother began to cry. "I can't run with these old legs!"

Thandiwe knew that her grandfather wouldn't be able to run either.

She saw the plant that her grandmother had brought with her from the homeland. It was in bloom for the first time. It was a wonderful plant, a sort of lily with flowers that made Thandiwe think of stars . . . white stars with red points. Grandmother said it was a very special plant.

"Yiza, Tatamkhulu! Yiza, Makhulu! Come, Grandfather! Come, Grandmother!"

Thandiwe grasped their hands and led them out of the house.

"What are you doing, my child?" her grandmother asked, and her grandfather's hand shook as he held onto his stick.

"Lindani apha, Tatamkhulu noMakhulu! Wait here!"

Then she ran into the house again and fetched the plant with its stand. The iron stand was heavy and she had to drag it.

She heard the bakkie's roar but she didn't look up. She put the plant upright in front of her. It stood right in the middle of the road.

When the bakkie got closer, she still couldn't see the men's faces. She stood with her legs astride, and clutched her grandparents' rough hands in her sweaty ones.

Her grandfather and grandmother asked no more questions. They just looked at her in the same way they looked when she took them to the post office or the Lucky Star Trading Store.

Thandiwe was frightened, but it was as if the plant with its flowers like stars gave her courage.

The bakkie stopped. She smelt the petrol fumes and felt the heat of its engine. Now she could see the four sweaty faces. The bakkie was full of iron sheets and wire.

Thandiwe lifted the plant from its stand. She went round to the driver's side with it in her arms. She held it up to him.

"Take the plant," she said. "But don't break down my grandparents' house."

The bakkie's engine shuddered and died.

The driver and the three other men looked at her. She smiled, but it wasn't her real smile.

"Go on!" she said. "Take the plant!"

No one said a word. She stared hard at them.

The driver struggled to start the engine.

"Where will it all end?" her grandmother asked as the bakkie revved and jerked away. Thandiwe was quiet for a long while. Then she spoke: "Look, Makhulu, the flowers look like stars. There won't always be darkness."

The people of Khayalethu Camp who had hidden in the bushes nearby saw the bakkie drive away. They couldn't understand it. All they could see was a young girl standing in the road with her grandparents behind her, and a plant with pretty flowers held close against her chest.   DH

LESLEY BEAKE
Giving

ILLUSTRATED BY NIKKI JONES

''WHAT ARE YOU GETTING?'' It was Bryce again. Jannie went on clearing his desk. He wished Bryce would disappear.

"I'm getting a BMX," Bryce boasted. "That's my main present, but I expect I'll be getting a crash-helmet and cycling shorts and that sort of thing as well."

Jannie reached right to the back of his desk. Where did all this stuff come from? He looked in disgust at what had been a sandwich – on the first day of the first term. This was the last day of the last term and Meneer Venter had told them to empty their Standard Three desks while he marked papers.

"So what *are* you getting?"

Jannie sighed. A clear picture of what Christmas would be like in Ouma's house came to his mind. He already knew what his present would be. Ouma had been skimping a rand at a time off the egg money for months to pay for it. It was a school raincoat. He knew because he had seen it in Yudelman's shop with a note pinned to it, saying it was to be kept for Mrs Van Straten.

He could almost hear what she would say when he opened the parcel: "You may as well have something you really need. And you wouldn't have had so many colds last winter if you'd had one then."

It was navy blue and too big so he would have room to grow. It was horrible!

"I don't know," Jannie answered Bryce, trying not to seem interested. "I'd like a new soccer ball, but my gran might have got me something else."

A faint smile of pity crossed Bryce's face.

"Ja. It must be tough living with an old stick like her."

"Ja." It was. Jannie felt the anger again. Why did his parents have to be dead?

But Bryce changed the subject. "You going to the braai?"

The braai was the Christmas function held every year by the factory where Bryce's father worked. Nearly everyone in their class had a father who worked there. Jannie had once had one too. Before the accident with the truck.

"Ja." He was going. Ouma said he must. "Your father would have liked you to go, Jannie."

"Well . . ." Bryce was getting ready to move off – thank goodness. "I've got to go. Japie Nel's giving me a chance on his BMX in the playground. Got to practise so I'm ready for the big day!"

Jannie thought he hated Bryce at that moment.

The braai was on Christmas Eve. Jannie tried to pretend he was sick, but he knew it was no good before he even started. "You'll be fine when you get there," Ouma said. "Your father wouldn't have let a little thing like a headache put him off when people were expecting him. When people had gone to trouble for him."

Why, Jannie wondered, did Ouma always manage to make him feel guilty?

Bryce was right at the door of the hall. He was zooming around on an imaginary bike, as if he already had his BMX.

"Hi, Jannie!"

"Hullo, Bryce."

"I found out I'm also getting a video machine. It's from my grandparents. They're really rich. They said they want me to watch educational videos." Bryce laughed in a way that told Jannie he wouldn't be watching many of *them.*

Jannie wandered around the hall for a while, but he wasn't interested in the other kids. He wasn't hungry for party-food and he had a real headache now. Maybe if he sneaked off round the corner of the stage behind the Christmas tree, nobody would notice . . . But when he got there, the hiding place was already occupied.

She was about five years old, wearing a crumpled pink-and-blue party dress and matching pink-and-blue shoes. And she was crying.

"Eh . . . why are you crying?" Jannie didn't have much experience with girls. "It can't be that bad."

He offered her his handkerchief and patted her a bit on the arm as if that might comfort her. It took a while, but eventually he found out what had caused the misery.

"I haven't got anything to *give* anybody!" she said. "It's Christmas, and I haven't got anything to *give*."

It hit Jannie like a thunderbolt. Of course! Here he was snivelling on about getting a raincoat – and missing the point entirely. He was just as bad as Bryce, now he came to think about it.

The lights on the tree flashed red and blue, yellow and green, and the smell of pine needles pricked his nose. And suddenly Jannie remembered the days before Christmas in his own home, when his parents had still been there . . . the rustle of gift-wrapping behind closed doors . . . the small gifts he used to make for his father and mother . . .

"Look," he said to the little girl, "you've got something you can give. Easy."

She looked at him doubtfully.

"What have you got lots of? Apart from tears."

She shook her head.

"Something you make with your mouth."

"Words?"

Jannie thought this was rather typical of a girl.

"No, man, something nicer."

And then she got it. "Smiles!"

"Right! Just give everyone one of them."

The one she gave him right then was dazzling.

This joy was with him still on Christmas morning when he gave Ouma the hot-water bottle he'd saved up for.

"Because I know how you feel the cold at night when winter comes," he explained.

Ouma smiled. "Ja, Jannie. Thank you, my boy. It will be very . . . useful."

But *her* parcel, when she gave it to him, didn't look useful at all. It didn't look a bit like a raincoat. Not unless she'd put something inside it to make it look like a . . . soccer ball!

"It's a raincoat," Jannie said firmly to himself as he undid the paper. "It's a navy blue raincoat." But he knew it wasn't.

"Thanks, Ouma!" were the only words he was able to get out. But his smile said everything else for him. "Can I go and play with it now?"

"Ja, Jannie. Enjoy it, and – happy Christmas!"

Bryce was circling around on a bike that sparkled so much that it almost hurt the eyes. Jannie didn't really even see it.

"What did you get then?"

Jannie forced his voice to be calm. "Soccer ball," he said briefly. "Like I said."

Bryce cast an experienced eye over the black-and-white ball. "Oh," he said, "I got one of those in Standard One."

LARRAINE KRIEK
QRT – a robot with a plan

ILLUSTRATED BY MEL TODD

TESS STOOD OUTSIDE the living room door with her rag doll in her hand. She was too frightened to go in. There was a . . . robot inside! She had only set eyes on him once – the day her father brought him back from America for Tim – but she knew exactly what he looked like: a barrel that was flattened on the sides and in front. He moved on three invisible wheels. There were a whole lot of buttons on his chest and his head was like half a pumpkin that could turn. His mouth looked like a mouth-organ with a light inside and he had an antenna on his head!

The robot also had two arms with grabbers at the ends. Tim said they were pincers, but she knew they were grabbers. Hungry grabbers!

Tess heard Tim speaking: "Do you hear me, QRT?"

"Deep . . . deep . . . I don't hear. I receive sound commands with my sensors." The robot's words came out jerkily, with a tinny sort of echo.

Tess opened the door. Tim would see that the robot wouldn't pinch her with its pincers or grab her with its grabbers. She didn't look at the robot and she held her hands over her doll's eyes. "Don't look, Gretel."

"Is your doll afraid of the robot too?" Tim laughed.

"Oh, Tim," Tess complained, "you play all day long with that horrible thing!"

She sat down on the broad window-seat. The curtain felt as soft and woolly as Aunt Hester's mother cat that had the four kittens. Outside in the garden she could see the wind blowing, pulling and plucking at the plants.

"Tess, let me show you how to programme the robot," Tim said.

"No! I want to learn how to tie bows and do magic . . . that's all."

Stupid girl, thought Tim. Once you're ten, you'll know that people can't do magic.

"Come on, just give him one command," he begged.

Tess didn't look at the robot but she said: "QRT, stand on your head!"

The robot's lights flickered red. "Deep . . . deep . . . command received. I am not a clown. I am programmed to solve problems."

Tim laughed. "Did you think he worked in the circus in America?"

Their mother came into the room. "Is it night-time already?" Tess asked. "Will Daddy be home soon?"

"No, it's still early, but there's a storm coming. The thunderclouds have made it dark. I'm just going across the way to help Aunt Hester shut her windows. It's hard for her in her wheelchair."

Tess saw that the clouds looked like thick puffy quilts. A window banged somewhere. She ran down the passage. It was her mother's bedroom window. She climbed onto the sill, stuck her hand through the burglar bars and shut the window.

The wooden floor made creaking sounds under her feet as she walked to the door. She turned the key in the lock. She wanted to try on some of her mother's make-up, and she didn't want Tim to bother her. She wasn't tall enough to reach the light switch but it didn't matter. There was still enough light left to see by.

She sat in front of the dressing-table. "Good morning, Madam!" she said to her reflection, and spattered a few drops of perfume on her arm.

Perhaps she'd look more grown-up with lipstick on. She rubbed some on her lips, powdered her face and put some blusher on her cheeks. Then she tried to smear some blue eye-shadow over her eyelids, but it was difficult. When she closed one eye, the other one closed as well.

Now she just needed a little black on her eyelashes. Or was it eyebrows? She always got muddled between the two.

Suddenly there was a crash of thunder. The whole house seemed to shake. Tess jumped with fright. She ran to the door. But when she tried to unlock it, the key was stuck fast.

It was very dark in the room already and she couldn't reach the light switch. "Tim! Tim!" she called, and banged the door until her hand was sore. At last she heard Tim on the other side: "Tess, what's the matter?"

Her throat was so choked up with tears that she couldn't speak. Tim tried turning the doorknob. "Have you locked the door and now you can't open it?" he asked.

"Y. . .es!" she sniffled.

"Tess, pull the key out. I'll fetch it at the window and unlock the door from this side."

She managed to get the key out and handed it to him through the window. The horrible old robot was with him!

"Talk to QRT while I go and unlock the door. And why does your face look like a paint advert?" Tim asked. Then he disappeared around the corner of the house. A few seconds later she heard him at the door, fiddling with the key.

Tess stared at the robot. "I wish you'd rust in the rain," she said.

The robot's lights flickered red. "Deep . . . deep . . . I am made from stainless steel. Stainless steel does not rust." Then his antenna wiggled backwards and forwards, almost as if he were laughing.

Tim came back around the corner of the house. He looked cross. "I can't open the door, Tess! What did you do to the lock?"

What if no one could open the door! Then she'd have to sleep in the big dark room all by herself. She was frightened of storms in any case. And her mother's shower curtain seemed to be moving.

She stared hard at the robot. Her father said that a robot should be *used*. They were there to help. Then suddenly she had an idea: "Tim, ask the robot what we should do!"

"QRT, the door is locked and the key is stuck in the lock. What shall we do?" Tim asked.

The robot's lights flickered green. "Deep . . . deep . . . Put oil on. Motor oil, furniture oil, cooking oil, castor oil, bath oil . . . deep . . . deep . . ."

"Bath oil?" asked Tess. "There's bath oil in Mom's bathroom. I'll go and fetch it."

She handed the oil to Tim through the window.

"Go and wash your face, Tess. QRT and I will rescue you," Tim teased. The robot wiggled his antenna again. Could he perhaps be laughing?

She rinsed her face in the bathroom. It was pitch dark. The thunder crackled and crashed and the creaking floor made her scared as well . . . something was lying on a chair . . . a strange bundle. It looked . . . as if . . . as if it moved! She froze. Tim was still fiddling with the key.

But just when she wanted to yell, the door burst open. Tim switched the light on. When you are ten, you can reach light switches and ice-suckers in the freezer, Tess thought.

"Thank you, Tim!" She felt quite weak with relief.

"Don't thank me. Thank QRT for solving the problem. And your face isn't clean yet! The paint has just moved about. The red is all around your mouth and your cheeks are smeared with blue and black. What does she look like, QRT?"

QRT's lights flickered green and red. "Deep . . . deep . . . unidentified object . . . possibly something from outer space or possibly a local spectacle . . . deep . . . deep . . ."

His antenna wiggled again. Was he laughing at her?

"I can't wash my face with soap. My eyes will burn." She looked at the robot. "How shall I clean my face, QRT?" Tess asked.

His lights flickered green and he said: "Deep . . . deep . . . oil. Not motor oil, or furniture oil, or cooking oil. Preferably castor oil or bath oil."

Tess saw that his antenna was wiggling again. Could he really be laughing?

"Come, I'll help you. I've just heard Dad's car," Tim said. In the bathroom he put some bath oil on a piece of cotton wool and wiped her face, just as he'd seen his mother

cleaning her face. When he was finished, her face was clean but quite shiny.

"Where are you hiding?" their mother called.

Tess ran down the passage and Tim and QRT followed. Their father came in through the front door. He picked her up. "Hmm, you smell nice, but you're very shiny and greasy," he said as he wiped her cheek. "Tim, switch off the robot's movement so that the battery doesn't run flat."

They told their father all about the key and QRT's plan. He said that the key did sometimes get stuck. You had to pull it out a little before turning it. But the oil had been a good idea.

Suddenly their mother fumbled in one of the large pockets of her jacket. "Look what I have for you, Tess!" She took out a small grey-striped kitten.

"A kitten from Aunt Hester's cat! Oh, isn't he sweet!" Tess pressed it under her chin.

"Yes, he was terrified of the storm and ran up a tree. I've been struggling to get him down all this time, until Dad came. He helped get him down. And then Aunt Hester said you could have him."

"I'm pleased we could rescue the kitten and that QRT could rescue you," her father said. "Where is the hero now?"

The robot was still standing in the passage. Tess heard him saying: "The hero is . . . deep . . . deep . . . in trouble. The movement mechanism is switched off."

Tess walked across to the robot and pressed the black button that made him move forward. "Poor robot," she whispered.

The robot rolled towards Tess's mother. "Deep . . . deep . . . could I have the kitten? Everyone has a pet except me."

"No," said Tess, "it's my kitten, but you can hold it for a while."

Tess's mother laughed. "You wouldn't be able to get the kitten out of a tree, QRT," she said. "I think Tim should buy you a goldfish tomorrow. How about that?"

The robot's lights flickered green. "Deep . . . deep . . . thank you, Mom," he said.

His pumpkin-head turned towards Tess. "Deep . . . deep . . . a little fish for a robot and a little kitten for an oily goil."

Tess laughed. "I'm not a goil, QRT! I'm a girl!"

QRT's antenna started shaking wildly.

Then Tess *knew* that he was laughing.

DH

DONALD RIEKERT
Crow's good-luck stone

ILLUSTRATED BY ELIZABETH ANDREW

EARLY THAT MORNING the rooster crowed cock-a-doodle-doo! from his perch in the vaalbos-tree near the cooking shelter.

Tshego threw off her blankets and opened the door. She stood in the doorway and watched the sun roll over the edge of the Phakela hills and sprinkle gold across the veld around Magonajeng.

Tshego felt eager for this day that broke so red over the hills. Who could tell? Perhaps this was the day money would come from her father. What if he came himself . . .? She laughed and clapped her hands. Her father always said: "Tshego has the right name. She is always laughing." He used to make up words and games which made her laugh. Her father could make her feel happy all day long.

But now her father had gone. One evening, he had spoken to her gently next to the cooking shelter. The flames from the burning vaalbos logs danced in his dark eyes. He took her hands in his. "Tshego," he said, "the mines are paying people off. They say no one wants to buy asbestos any longer. I'm going to work in the city. An old foreman of mine has asked me to come."

At first her father used to send money, but after a while it had stopped coming. If only he wasn't ill, Tshego thought. Her mother and her grandmother had become quiet. The money had run out. There was hardly any food left in the house. Her mother had walked the streets looking for work in town but had found nothing.

Tshego stood and watched the sun climb higher over the hills. In spite of her worries, she smiled – what was Crow doing this morning? Her father had found the little crow chick in the veld. "You must teach it to talk and laugh," he had said. Her grandmother had fed it worms and flies. Crow had grown tame quickly and followed Tshego everywhere.

Suddenly there he was. He came flying down and flapped to the ground next to her feet. Tshego's eyes opened wide. Something was shining in the bird's beak – a small bright stone as big as the tip of her little finger.

"Grandmother, come and see!" Tshego called.

Her grandmother shuffled out of the house. She looked in surprise at the crow which was walking around Tshego with the bright stone in its beak. "Crow's stone is a good-luck stone!" she said, and laughed for the first time in many days. She bent down and took the shiny stone out of the crow's beak and looked at it for a long while. "Look, Tshego," she said, "this crystal has smooth, flat sides. You don't find this kind often. Look after it well."

Tshego picked up a scrap of paper. She wrapped it around the stone and put it safely into her pocket.

Suddenly she had an idea: Why shouldn't she too collect crystals, and sell them? She'd heard the children talking about a man in town who bought pretty stones. The children said he made little trees from twisted copper wire and stones of many different colours. They stood in his shop window.

She knew that just behind the hill, near Seodin, there were beautiful crystal stones among the trassie-bushes. She and her father used to walk there on Sundays. He used to sit and stare out over the veld for a long time while she played house, and that's when she'd seen the stones under the trassie-bushes.

As soon as she'd eaten her porridge, she took an old mealie-bag from the cooking shelter. She found the head of a broken pick and off she went.

A few crystals lay scattered about, but there were others that she had to break loose with the pick. The sweat ran into her eyes and her arms ached. When she'd collected enough, she decided to take them to town straight away. But she hadn't noticed how low the sun had sunk.

Tshego struggled to sling the bag over her shoulder and began walking. But the bag was heavy and she stumbled. Just then she heard the sound of a donkey-cart behind her and looked back. It was their neighbour. He stopped.

"Dumela, Tshego."

"Dumela, Uncle."

"Climb up, Tshego. Where are you going?"

"I'm going to town, Uncle. I must sell these stones. There's no more food at home."

"Ai, ai, Tshego, let me help you load the stones onto the cart."

Tshego talked happily about her father while the donkey-cart's wheels hummed over the sandy road.

"I'll drop you off near the shop," the old man said as they rode into town. "But I wonder if you're not a little too late, Tshego. When you're finished, come and meet me here at the turn-off."

He helped Tshego load the bag onto her shoulder. She was a little frightened because she didn't often come to town.

When she got to the stone-shop, she saw the small wire trees in the window, but the shop was closed!

A boy passed by. She asked him if he knew of another place where she could sell stones. The boy pointed to a large house against the hill. "Try Ditedu . . . the man with a beard. Perhaps he'll be able to help. He's the man from Blouberg mine."

Tshego gathered her courage again and struggled on with her bag of stones towards the house. The shadows were making long stripes already. She would have to hurry.

What if the man with the beard was fierce?

She stood in front of the gate. A small boy was sitting on a low wall, patting his collie's head. He seemed a little younger than she was.

He looked up. "Dumela," she said softly.

"Dumela," he answered.

"Ditedu o kae? Where is Ditedu?"

The boy laughed. "The beard-man will be coming soon. I'm also waiting for him."

Tshego sat down facing him. "My name is Max," he said. "My father is the manager of Blouberg Asbestos."

Tshego looked up at the house against the hill. "My name is Tshego," she said. "You've got a big house!"

Max's face suddenly grew sad. "My father says we're going to lose everything," he said. "Then it won't be our house any more. Blouberg Asbestos is closing. My father says we'll have to move. Lots of people have moved away already."

Tshego stared at the boy. "My father has gone away too. Now we have no food in our house."

"And my father . . ." Max said, ". . . I have to stay away from him. He shouts at me for nothing. It's because of the mine closing. He hasn't a job any more."

Max took a large white envelope from his shirt pocket. "Look here, Tshego, it's from my grandmother. I'm seven today." He took the card out of its envelope. It showed a boy sailing a boat on a fish-pond.

"Happy birthday," Tshego said. "I'm eight

already." She opened the bag to show Max the crystals. They were looking at them when a big car drove through the gate and swung up the driveway. Tshego saw it was the man with the beard. She held on to the bag anxiously. He looked so fierce!

The man climbed out of the car and walked towards them. He smiled. "Max, it's your birthday, my boy!" He picked him up and threw him into the air three times. Max shouted with laughter.

Then his father put him down and asked: "Who's your friend?"

"I'm selling stones." Tshego spoke quickly, and turned the stones out of the bag.

"They're the stones that Uncle Jim always buys, Dad, but his shop is closed."

Max's father didn't reply.

Suddenly everything seemed too much for Tshego. Her eyes filled with tears.

"Dad," Max said, "I've got Grandma's birthday money. I could buy the stones. Can I, Dad?"

Max's father looked surprised. Then his eyes softened. "Buy them if you want to, my boy. Perhaps you can make a small profit when you sell them to Uncle Jim tomorrow. They're beautiful crystals."

Max pulled his grandmother's gift from the envelope. Tshego took the ten-rand note from him and put it into her pocket. She smiled. Then she fumbled in her pocket again, brought out a small bundle of paper and opened it. She looked down at the crow's good-luck stone. "It's pasela," she said, and gave it to Max. "A present for you. It will bring you good luck."

His father picked up the crystal from Max's hand. "It's a perfect crystal. You seldom get one like this," he said. "And I think the good luck may have started already. It looks as though we will be able to stay here after all – I was offered a job in the town today."

Max smiled at Tshego, because he knew that he had just been given the best birthday present ever.

Tshego picked up the empty bag. "Dumela," she said. "Next week, when I bring stones to the shop again, I'll come to see if you're still here, Max!"

DH

MARETHA MAARTENS
Red cooldrink

ILLUSTRATED BY NIKKI JONES

"WHEN ARE YOU GOING to buy a new lorry, Grampa?" Freddy asked. Behind them cars were hooting. Grampa's lorry had stalled again at the traffic light.

"This old lorry is perfect," Grampa said as he lifted the bonnet, fiddled around a little in the engine and then climbed back in. "Just watch this." He turned the ignition key and the engine took.

BRRRRMMM . . . the lorry revved. BRRRRMMM . . .

"The people are fed-up," Freddy said as he glanced out of the back window. "Look at the hundreds of cars behind us, Grampa."

BRRRRMMM! Grampa revved the engine once more.

"You're making too much noise, Grampa." He felt embarrassed. "New lorries don't struggle like this."

"New lorries cost money," Grampa replied. The light changed to green again and they shuddered forward.

"When you're finished building for Mr Mothobi, then you'll have enough money."

Grampa scratched around in the cubby-hole and pulled out a packet of raisins. "Help yourself, then pour some in my hand as well," he said.

Freddy chewed slowly on the fat brown raisins.

"Do you remember what we said about choices?" Grampa suddenly asked.

Freddy spat out a pip. The lorry was old. Grampa didn't mind the raisin pips.

"You said that every time a person makes a choice, it costs something."

"It's like that now," said Grampa. "When I get my money from Mr Mothobi, I have to choose what to do with it. If I choose to buy a new lorry then I can't afford to buy that retirement house for Grandma and me."

"More raisins, Grampa?" Freddy asked.

Grampa held his hand out for another little mound of raisins. "Now I'm choosing to have a stomach like a beer-barrel," he said. "Look how many raisins I'm gobbling."

"Well, if you don't take some, you're choosing to let your stomach growl."

"Hmmm?"

"When you long for something and you don't get it, then your stomach growls," Freddy said. "It happened to me once in church. I sat and thought about puddings and grrr, my stomach growled. Everyone laughed at me."

"Here we are," said Grampa, as he stopped in front of a large new building. "Today we lay carpets. I hope my back can take it. There's Luka already."

Freddy and Luka had become friends while the building was going up. Luka could do absolutely anything. He could stand on his head, walk on his hands, coo-coorrrr just like a dove through a gap between his cupped hands, break an apple in half with his bare hands, and balance a two-rand piece on his nose and walk about without dropping it. He could take an alarm clock apart and put it together again, dive from the high board and speak Afrikaans.

Luka Mothobi was the best friend in the whole world.

89

But it was easy to be jealous of Luka. He made walking on his hands seem so simple that when Freddy tried and fell on his head, he just wanted to swear!

"The carpets are here," Luka said to Freddy. "They came in big fat rolls. One room is full of them."

"I brought my fighter-plane along," said Freddy.

"I brought mine too," Luka said. But he looked quickly over his shoulder. "Freddy, let's first go and play between all the rolls of carpet. There're tunnels and towers and places to creep through and places to jump from, and plenty of space to play."

"D'you think we're allowed?"

"My father didn't say anything," Luka replied.

Grampa and his helpers were busy carrying the first roll of carpet up the stairs to the top floor. "Hupp-hupp . . . hup-hu-u-u-uppp!" Freddy heard them calling out together. He and Luka rushed into the room where the rolls of carpet lay.

It was as Luka had said. Someone had dumped the carpets hurriedly: some rolls were lying flat and others were upright. There were plenty of places to jump from. The whole room smelt of new carpets, soft wool and a wonderful time.

"Whoo-ooo-ps!" shouted Luka as he flew like a swallow from the top of a pile and landed with a somersault onto a heap of fluffy mats. He lay on his back, laughing.

It looked such fun that Freddy also climbed up and spread his wings and flew.

While Grampa and his helpers were busy upstairs, Freddy and Luka flew and rolled and jumped and tumbled. They were birds and pilots and aeroplanes and angels, vampires and bats.

After a while Luka said: "I'm going to fetch some cooldrink."

"Where from?" asked Freddy.

"In our fridge. It's working already. We put

some bottles in last night." So Luka ran down the passage and came back with two bottles of cooldrink and a bottle opener.

"Are you sure we can just take it?" Freddy asked.

Luka nodded. He sat astride one of the rolls of carpet. Chkkk! He popped off the first bottle-top. Then he put the bottle of red cool-drink down on the carpet and propped it up with his leg. CHKKK! The second bottle-top popped off. But he had pulled too hard and the bottle slipped out of his hands.

Freddy just stared. All he saw was foam and red cooldrink. It flowed out of the bottle like a red waterfall and collected in red dams on the carpet around Luka.

"Luka!" he whispered.

"Oh, blast!" Luka exclaimed.

"Grampa's going to lay into us!" said Freddy.

"I don't cry for anything," said Luka as he tried to mop up the cooldrink with his shirt.

I always cry when I get a hiding, Freddy thought. It's like going to the dentist or get-ting an injection against measles. Don't be a cry-baby, Grampa always says . . .

I don't want to cry in front of Luka! Oh, blast! I really don't want to cry in front of him!

Just then Grampa and Luka's father ap-peared at the door.

Grampa gave one look. "Off!" he growled.

Mr Mothobi gave three looks. "Ako nthuse hle, ntate! Please help me, father!" he said as he looked at Grampa. His face seemed to get bigger and bigger, like a balloon that was be-ing blown up with plenty of breath.

And Grampa's face became redder and red-der. "We'll have to get people in to clean the carpet," he said. "What a disaster!"

"These children need a jolly good hiding," Mr Mothobi said.

"I've a heart problem," said Grampa. "You punish them, Mr Mothobi. Your hands are strong enough."

"I won't cry," said Luka suddenly.

Mr Mothobi looked Luka in the eye. "I don't want to make you cry. I want to make you feel. If children won't think with their heads, then they must feel it on their bottoms."

And suddenly Freddy saw Mr Mothobi's strong hands come towards him. Smackkk . . . smackkk . . . slap . . . smackkk!

I must *not* cry! thought Freddy, but tears began to spill over his cheeks and run down his nose.

Suddenly Luka dashed past.

"Luka!" Mr Mothobi shouted after him, and let go of Freddy.

But Luka was already outside and up a tree.

I only got four smacks, Freddy thought. Four smacks weren't much: a person could just sniff back the tears.

"Come down from there!" Mr Mothobi said.

"Leave him, Mr Mothobi," said Grampa. "Look! He's already had his hiding."

Luka was crying as if he'd had *fifteen* smacks.

"Come down, Luka," Grampa urged, and put his arms out to help him down. Luka climbed down slowly and clung onto Grampa like a cat. Grampa helped him to the ground and glanced at Mr Mothobi.

"The two of you go and play," he said to Freddy and Luka.

Freddy felt like saying: Luka doesn't cry for anything – he cries for nothing! But then he remembered what Grampa had said about choices. You must choose what you say. Luka wasn't really brave after all, but he was still his best friend.

He snapped his mouth shut. When he opened it again, other words spilled out: "There's a dung beetle's hole under the blue-gum tree."

Luka looked hard at him. "If we catch it, I'll harness it to a leaf for you," he said. "You'll see. The beetle will pull the leaf just like a wagon."

"Then we'll pack little stones on the wagon," Freddy said.

"And build a factory," said Luka.

"A cooldrink factory," said Freddy.

"And we'll drink plenty of cooldrink!" said Luka with a smile.

"Red cooldrink!" Freddy laughed.

"Red cooldrink that squirts out!" Luka shouted.

And they ran to dig the dung beetle out of its hole.

DH

KASIYA MAKAKA

Kakhuni in the Valley of Lasting Dew

ILLUSTRATED BY CORA COETZEE

KAKHUNI, WHOSE NAME MEANS "Little-Tree" in the language of northern Malawi, was a cowherd, shepherd and goatherd. He looked after two cows, two sheep and two goats. He lived with his grandmother in a village overlooking the Great Rift Valley.

Kakhuni had something no other shepherd possessed: a club made of ebony, left to him by his great-grandfather. It was no ordinary club either – it was a magic club.

Every morning Kakhuni got up early to pack his breakfast of sour milk and roast sweet potatoes and ground-nut butter. Then he would take his ebony club from under his pillow and go out quietly while his grandmother slept.

Outside it would be dark still and the morning star would be very bright in the east. The Rift Valley would be one white blanket of fog and the many valleys of Kavhuzi lay laced in thin veils of mist, waiting for the herds.

Each herd knew its valley and would graze there all day. Kakhuni's herd always went to the furthest valley. First along the main ridge, then down the valley of banana gardens, past the orange groves, past the peach orchards, past the cassava ridge into the wide and deep rice valley. And then finally, as the first rays of the rising sun reached the ridges of Kavhuzi, Kakhuni and his six animals would descend into the Valley of Lasting Dew.

On the other side of the Valley of Lasting Dew was the Forest of Final Rest, where the people of the high plain of Kavhuzi were buried. Of all the forests, the Forest of Final Rest was the biggest and densest and no child was allowed to enter it. The children were told that they would disturb the spirits of the dead.

Many shepherds knew that the Valley of Lasting Dew had much good grass and herbs that cattle and goats and sheep liked. They knew that the dew was good for their animals, but they would not go there. The spirits, they said, wash their hands and feet in the dew early in the morning and late in the afternoon.

Kakhuni knew all this. He was careful never to get to the Valley of Lasting Dew too early in the morning. And he and his well-fed herd never stayed in the valley till too late in the afternoon.

But because the Valley of Lasting Dew was so far away, it was always dusk when Kakhuni got back to the ridge where he and his grandmother lived. And ever so often his grandmother would say to him: "Oh, Little-Tree, never stay late in the grazing grounds. These valleys are full of spirits."

Early one morning Kakhuni got up as usual to pack his breakfast. It was a day like all other days – so Kakhuni thought, as he listened to the distant whistling of shepherds, goatherds and cowherds. The morning breeze carried the crack of soft sisal whips to his ears. The day had started, and goats and sheep and cattle were moving slowly towards the valleys of Kavhuzi.

Kakhuni set off for the Valley of Lasting Dew and got there, as usual, just as the gazelles were going to rest in the warmth of the Forest of Final Rest.

At the edge of the valley Kakhuni said a little prayer:

"Spirits of our fathers
spirits of the vast world
protect my feet in this old valley
protect my herd
I am your child –
a son of the grassy ridges of Kavhuzi."

And so he let his flock of two sheep, his herd of two cows and his two goats graze. The grass was rich everywhere, so the animals never wandered far.

Kakhuni went to a little rise and lay down on his back to rest his legs. Then he took the little calabash in which he carried his sour milk and placed it carefully in front of him. He unwrapped the ground-nut butter he carried wrapped in banana leaves and loosened the thin tree-bark string which had kept his roast sweet potatoes nicely tied together. He ate his breakfast slowly and quenched his thirst from the little calabash.

Then he took out his bamboo flute and played simple, pleasant tunes on it. For a while he tried to imitate the sounds made by the forest birds. They all sounded so simple but were so hard to imitate. But then he tired of trying to copy bird-calls and put his flute away. He started running about the lush grass, kicking the dew with his feet, laughing at the showers of glistening drops set free by his movements.

When he finally stopped and looked around, the goats and the sheep had disappeared.

He hurried back to the little rise and searched the wide valley with his sharp eyes. No goats. No sheep. Only the two cows.

He picked up his magic ebony club and hit the ground fiercely – once and twice and then three times – and cried:

"Zimnyama, great son of the plains, I knock at your door, son of the earth. Tell me, where have my sheep gone? Tell me, where have my goats gone?"

He listened. He thought he heard the sheep bleating. He closed his eyes and danced round and round, all the time swinging his ebony club, until he felt dizzy. He fell down, opened his eyes and looked to see in which direction his club was pointing. That was the direction the sheep must have taken.

So Kakhuni herded his cows in that direction. His sharp eyes searched the grass in front and to the sides. Suddenly he heard a clear sound of bleating.

"My sheep!" he exclaimed – and there they were, lying down in the grass. But where were the goats?

This time Kakhuni swung the ebony club above his head and let it go. The club sailed high through the air and came back to where he was. It pointed towards a little forest to one side of the Forest of Final Rest. The goats must have gone there.

So Kakhuni herded his cows and sheep towards the little forest. His eyes searched. His ears listened. It was getting late and even the birds which had sung all day had grown quieter.

When Kakhuni got to the edge of the little forest, he felt himself drawn to go in.

"Zimnyama, father of my father's father, protect me in the little forest," he prayed.

Then he went in, leaving his cows and sheep all tied to trees on the edge of the forest. He closed his eyes for a short while to listen to his inner voice. When he opened them again – what a sight met them! Mushrooms! Blue, green, yellow, bright red, orange – mushrooms of all colours.

Kakhuni stopped with his mouth open. He had never seen so many brightly coloured mushrooms before. He fell down on his knees and stroked the mushrooms. He stroked the large ones and the tiny button-sized ones. "Mushrooms . . ." he whispered. "This is the Forest of Mushrooms! I am lucky! I can make

a wish. I wish . . . I wish I could grow up and be given a wife as loving as my grandmother."

He closed his eyes, and when he opened them he was on the edge of the little forest, untying his cows and sheep and . . . The goats were there too! But Kakhuni was not surprised. He simply gathered them and herded them homeward.

It was very late and everywhere there were sounds. Behind him the little forest grew dark. And darker still grew the Forest of Final Rest, from where unearthly sounds seemed to reach out for his ears like long fingers. The grass in the Valley of Lasting Dew grew wetter and heavier and seemed to be holding fast his legs and those of his animals. They could not walk quickly. Everything was slipping away into darkness – and Kakhuni was still in the valley. He felt more and more tired and sleepy.

With weary arms he lifted his club and feebly he whispered: "Zimnyama, greatgrandfather . . ." – he had to stop to fight the drowsiness – "show me the way . . ." He was almost falling down from fatigue when at last he managed to say: ". . . home."

And suddenly Kakhuni felt himself being pulled as if by a hand. His club! It seemed to be tugging at his hand. And he felt his feet grow a bit lighter, although they still felt heavy and weary.

Finally, after what seemed a whole night, Kakhuni got to the ridge that guarded the Valley of Lasting Dew. He looked back and saw that the thin veil which always sealed off the valley at night had already covered half of it, and long strands of mist were reaching out like thin, bony fingers – reaching for his eyes, his ears, his legs.

But the club seemed to be tugging at Kakhuni's hand and urging him on, and as the fingers of mist reached the bottom of the ridge, he and his animals descended into the deep and wide valley of rice fields.

On they trudged, up to the ridge of cassava fields, to the peach orchards, the orange groves, then past the banana gardens and on to the main ridge . . . and finally to the safety of home.

"Oh, Little-Tree, never ever stay so late in the grazing grounds again. These valleys are full of spirits!"

At the sound of his grandmother's voice, the ebony club dropped from Kakhuni's hand and he collapsed from fatigue. His grandmother half carried, half dragged him inside. She drove the animals to their shelter, and then she sat down at Kakhuni's side and waited for him to start speaking.

She waited.

All night she waited.

But Kakhuni, who was in a deep sleep, did not wake up until late the following day. "Oh, Grandmother," he said, "if it weren't for my ebony club . . ."

And then he told her what had happened in the Valley of Lasting Dew the night before.